Gradient Descent
Schrödinger's Dog
Jim Christopher

https://www.daftinstitute.com

Published by Jim Christopher.

ISBN-13: 978-1-958855-00-3 (e-book)

ISBN-13: 978-1-958855-01-0 (paperback)

Cover design by MIBLArt.

First edition, published 16 May 2023

To all the amazing women
who continue working in science and technology
despite most of the men
working in science and technology.

Nothing in life is to be feared, it is only to be understood. Now is the time to understand more, so that we may fear less.

— Marie Curie

Foresight

"I hate these dog and pony shows." Max was quiet, her voice just cresting the sensitive microphone at her lips. Yet Min heard the words as if they came from her own brain thanks to the lab's comms system.

"They're kind of fun," Min said into her own mic. "They're necessary, at least. These 'dog and pony' shows provide our 'bread and butter.'" *And our ticket out from under Waffel's thumb,* she thought. Her eyes stayed fixed on the telemetry in her terminal. "How are the power reserves?"

"Capacitors are humming at 94%."

"Nice." At that capacity, they should have enough juice to run the quantum telescope for almost 700 milliseconds. Enough for the live demonstration. Min's focus returned to the conversation in the auditorium.

Dr. Shauna Waffel stood on the stage, speaking to the small group of Department of Defense leadership and high-ranking technical staff. Her voice dripped with confidence, which Min recognized to be false. Dr. Waffel knew almost nothing about the physics behind quantum optics, and even less about the Foresight telescope. Yet Min's doctoral advisor and gatekeeper had no qualms about taking credit for both.

"The future of optics is quantum." An attractive and inaccurate CAD diagram of Foresight appeared on the one-story screen behind Waffel's hearty frame. Min sighed. Detail was missing from the infographic - stuff that was imperative to how Foresight operated, which Waffel decided was too deep for the brass to process. The professor continued, "Conventional optics rely on *capturing* light. It informs only on light we can reach. That light must have already touched something, matter absorbing some of its energy, bent across the cosmos by gravity and time, until it lands on an active sensor."

Min mouthed the words as they left her advisor's lips, matching each pause and raising her eyebrows on each syllable of emphasis. After the countless dry-runs, the late hours of rehearsal with Waffel, she knew the pitch by heart. The timings necessary to make the magic happen had become etched in the folds of her cortex. The first cue for the demonstration was approaching.

Waffel's overbearing voice returned. "The universe is full of light, yet statistically speaking, we are blind. Limited to the chance photons that are passing by when we are paying attention." The slide behind her changed to an animation: a countless number of orange particles, bouncing in random directions, representing photons. A thin cone of pale blue expanded across the screen, turning the specks it intersected white.

The first cue.

"Power the laser," Min breathed into her mic.

The clack of Max's mechanical keyboard preceded the safety lights darkening the window, letting anyone watching know not to approach without eye protection.

"Emitter is active," Max confirmed. "Capacitors at 92% and holding."

Min's eyes shifted to the monitor above her terminal. Four cameras showed the components of her Rube-Goldberg machine that crammed together conventional and quantum physics: the laser emitter spitting out the sickly green beam of light; the artificial quartz crystal that split the light into two entangled streams; the near-microscopic ring of exotic metal saddling one beam; and the complex and bulky array of conventional optics that transformed the second beam into a visible picture. A fifth camera captured the optical output from the entangled laser.

The presentation continued, with Waffel easing across the stage and snapping down her blazer. "But why limit ourselves to the light we capture? The Foresight project aims to turn this problem on its head." She moved to the right side of the stage. Behind her, the screen faded to white. A stagehand scooted into the frame, wheeling a large platform to the center of the stage. A red apple sat atop a plain ceramic pedestal at one end of the rolling surface. At the other end, a tripod squatted. It appeared to be empty, but Min knew what was there: a second aperture. Smaller than a grain of sand. Fabricated from the same strange material as the one in her telescope.

The stagehand sidled off-camera, hunching his shoulders as if to shrink out of the presentation. The screen reframed to include Waffel and her demonstration platform.

"Power status?" Min asked. The moment of truth was approaching.

Max answered without clacking her keyboard this time. "Holding at 91%. We're good to go on aperture use."

Min's hands flexed, her fingers wriggling out of their fists as they moved to her keyboard. The keys eased under her fingertips as she typed the command that would transfer almost two gigawatts of energy through the micrometer ring of the Foresight telescope. Eyes darting over each letter, she double- then triple-verified it was correct before moving her index finger over the ENTER key. She waited for Waffel to speak the next cue. The one to start the demo that would convince the DoD to fund Waffel for another five years. Prompt her advisor to approve Min's Ph. D. and recommend her for that sweet postdoctoral stint at JPL.

Waffel lingered behind the podium. "Say this apple is a state secret. Not one of ours, but our enemy's."

Min's heart skipped a beat. Waffel's words weren't right.

"Did you guys change the script?" Max sounded perturbed.

Min shook her head. *What the hell is Waffel doing?*

"Ah, Christ on a cracker, is she ad-libbing?" Max clacked on her keyboard. "Capacitors are at 90% now and dropping. She better get on with it."

Min's index finger twitched toward the key, wanting to press it. *Get to the second cue, you egotistical asshat!*

"The secret apple lives in a super-secure facility. No hope of getting access through espionage or force," Waffel said. Her thin lips turned down in a shallow expression of concern. "But why waste time and energy, or the lives of brave American patriots? With Foresight, we don't need to leave our chairs." Waffel's hands tapped the tablet on the podium, and the same camera feeds Min used to monitor Foresight appeared on the screen behind her. The stage washed in the pale green glow of the laser magnified on the large screen.

"Come on," Min begged, her mind and index finger writhing for Waffel to return to the script they had timed to perfection.

"86%," Max reported. "Falling fast. We're cutting it close."

"I'm aware," Min snapped, her anxiety overflowing. Four years of work were about to be destroyed by her advisor's need for drama.

"We are no longer constrained to the light we can see." Waffel's voice returned after a dramatic pause.

"She's back on script," Min sighed, her finger closing on the key. "Just keep those power levels up, Max."

"We're almost at 80%. Waffel's patriotic interlude may have cost us the demo, Min."

"No, no, no!" Min felt the tingle in her sinuses, the precursor to stress tears. At this level, the capacitors could dump around 1.3 gigawatts of power in a few milliseconds. A mind-boggling transfer of energy. Yet not enough to make the aperture perform.

"I can reconnect the feed from the nuclear plant," Max offered. "Try to goose the capacitors for a few seconds?"

"Do it!" The stress was causing Min to raise her voice, unnecessary with the microphone touching her mouth.

"Done," Max said as Waffel approached the final go-signal. "Capacitors at 82% and rising."

"That'll have to do." Min tried to copy Max's emotional control. "Prepare for power transfer."

"Okay," Max confirmed. "83%."

Waffel spoke, the words lost in the jumble of stress and panic bouncing against Min's skull. The professor's hand rose, her middle finger and thumb pressed together, building potential energy that she would release as a snap.

This was it: the signal to execute.

Min stared, unblinking. Holding her breath in her chest and her fingertip over the keyboard. Waiting for the percussive release of that finger snap. As Waffel's fingertip collided into the flesh of her thumb joint, Min mashed the ENTER key.

In microseconds, enough energy to power a small city moved into the ring of metal. For the next half-second, the aperture transferred that energy in and out of the beam, changing the light's physical and quantum states to mimic those passing through the aperture on the stage. The entangled beam of light reacted in kind, unable to resist the foundational laws of the universe. The lenses in the optical array pulled the narrow column of light apart. Isolated polarities. Recombined the photons into a microscopic image before they landed on the digital transducer feeding the camera.

She saw it. The visage of the apple on to her monitor. Eyes drifting to the presentation, she found the apple projected on the screen behind Waffel. Fuzzy, the color off, but recognizable. A beautiful, power-hungry still-life of fruit that cost ten times any Cezanne portrait. That two-story apple behind Waffel was proof that Foresight delivered. It was the lock on her doctorate, the bookend to Min's awful time working under Waffel at the Daft Institute. That nutritious-looking figure meant Min was moving on to better pastures.

You're a shooting star. That's all any of us are. The lyrics to her favorite song rang through Min's head.

"We're spiking." Max's voice remained a whisper. "Power draw is exceeding 2.5 gigawatts."

The words didn't register until the image of the apple disappeared from the auditorium screen. Min's cheeks slacked, her smile dissolving as she looked to her monitor. It was blank as well.

"Emergency shut down," Max reported. Her tone never broke its calm stride, the engineer maintaining her cool-as-a-cucumber vibe. "I can't stop it. Something's wrong, Min."

Min stood. The window into the clean room exploded with light, burning her eyes.

2

TRIP THE BREAKER

The lab went dark. No vomit-green ambiance. No warning lights. Then the standard wash of the overhead LEDs opened, bleeding into her saturated vision.

The women stayed silent and still for several seconds. Longer than the Foresight device had been active.

"What happened?" Min asked as she moved closer to the window. The apparatus appeared fine.

Max sighed, and her voice came through the air rather than Min's headset. "The capacitors drained, and the aperture kept pulling power straight from the fission reactor. We probably tripped the breaker."

Shit. "Tripping the breaker" was a euphemism for overdrawing their allotted power cycles. Daft's private nuclear plant could generate a sustained output of around three gigawatts. The individual labs and projects had to share that energy. With innovation came obscene power needs, so while the plant could deliver the energy needed to run Las Vegas, the demands of the Institute exceeded that by several factors. So, power consumption had to be scheduled. When you drew outside of your assigned times, there was a fine—either money or, more devastating, a debit against future power use.

Waffel's scolding grimace filled Min's head, then evaporated as an unfamiliar voice swelled into the lab. She turned from the window, finding the source.

"I don't understand." The rough baritone was coming from the desk. The auditorium presentation was still live. "Is it some kind of microscopic camera? Because we've had those for decades, Dr. Waffel." The man's tone was curt and impatient. Military brass expecting to be wowed with technology we could use to kill indiscriminate swaths of people, or a few specific individuals.

"No, General Gates, it's not a *camera.*" Waffel was struggling to maintain her authority, and Min could hear her discomfort and confusion. "As I stated, Foresight is a quantum telescope. It manipulates a local stream of photons to mimic another, across any distance."

"So it sees through walls?" the General asked.

"No," Waffel snapped. Her patience with the brass was fraying. "Sort of. But it does more than that!"

"Well then, explain it to us, doctor!" Now the General was losing his cool. "Explain why we're dumping fifty million dollars a year into-"

The speaker snipped as Max shut it off, leaving the control room in its natural state of eerie silence. The paneled walls of the Daft Institute comprised an acoustic-dampening polymer that absorbed almost all vibration, giving the wide area a stuffy quality.

Min's gaze rose to her lab partner. Max's stare was bright, and her face sported the thin half-smile of the cat that ate the canary.

Meanwhile, Min's stomach roiled. "How are you calm right now?"

The short woman's ruby grin widened into her cheeks, and her eyes piqued as she shrugged. "Because it's over. We did our part, Min. The demo worked."

"Technically," Min added. Her hand went to her head, brushing a strand of loose hair back into her ponytail. "It worked for a few hundred milliseconds."

"That's a success."

"Again, technically," Min repeated. "But Waffel will be upset the presentation wasn't perfect."

Max moved around the wide L-shaped desk they shared, stepping over the dog bed on the floor by her station. The bed belonged to Max's dog, Neils Bork; while the lab's mascot had passed away a few months ago, neither woman could bring themselves to remove the reminder of their friend. "When isn't she pissed?" Min felt her friend's hand reach the small of her back, Max turning Min toward the window overlooking the Foresight telescope. "But Waffel's presentation skills aren't under our control. It's not our job to sell the damned thing. All we do is make it work."

Min snorted as her eyes scanned the clean white lines of the telescope components. "All we do, huh? Makes it sound like a cakewalk." Her gaze traced the limb-sized power leads coming out of the floor, knowing they connected to an array of supercapacitors that occupied four square kilometers of space on the floor below them. The entire Foresight telescope sat on a workbench just large enough to eat a meal on. The hollow around that tiny table inside of the vast clean room carried a sudden girth. Her life's ambition sitting on a one-by-three meter surface, dwarfed by the cabling needed to power it. Her work felt diminutive at that moment. All her effort, surrounded by nothing and consuming energy like a kid eats candy.

"Come on, Eeyore," Max said. Her hand flipped to fingertips, poking Min towards the clean room doors. "After the brass chews her up, Waffel will want to know what happened. So let's figure it out."

Inside the clean room, Max moved to disconnect the telescope from the couplings. There was no danger of electrocution - the capacitor field was dry; however, the bundle of arm-thick cables suspended over the table by safety armatures prevented access to most of the Foresight components. Max unlocked the gimble and pushed her compact frame against the disconnected cables. The hanging armature shifted the bulk away from the telescope in a motion that reminded Min of the medical lights in a dentist's office.

She scanned the components on the workbench, evaluating them as a mother looking over an injured child. The minuscule aperture looked fine, still held by epoxy next to the quartz. She'd need a microscope to be sure, but the crystal itself appeared undamaged as well, its faceted surface smooth and transparent. Min's eyes tracked the path the light would take to the optical sensor.

Max crossed to the far side of the table. "Holy shit, how'd that happen?"

Min's procedural observation lost its focus, and she looked up to the engineer. "What?"

Max's eyebrows rose. She pointed to the optics. "That."

Min circled the table, her eyes following the line from Min's calloused finger to the optical components.

Her brow furrowed. Something had cracked the casing holding the optics, leaving a ragged hole several millimeters across. The polymer housing was necessary, since the mathematics behind conventional optics was unforgiving. While Min could fabricate the lenses to micrometer specifications, their positioning needed additional precision in order to elaborate the minuscule beam of entangled light back into a visible image.

"How's that possible?" she asked, looking at Max. The engineer was glancing from corner to corner, floor to ceiling.

"I don't think it is," Max said. "That polymer can withstand a bullet without getting a blemish. The stuff inside wouldn't even feel it happen."

"A fabrication defect?" Min offered.

"Maybe." Max sounded unconvinced. Her eyes landed back on the table and then raised to meet Min. "Something still had to strike it."

Min nodded.

Max held up a palm and gestured to the surrounding space. "So... what was it, then? Nothing in this room was moving."

3

Foreign Body

A line chiseled across Haoyu's forehead. He had the optical array on his workbench, secured with magnetic bench-dogs under the digital microscope. His attention remained fixed on the monitor displaying a few square microns of the casing.

"Preposterous," he concluded. "This is impossible, Min."

"You've said that several times, and yet..." Min gestured to the workbench. "I need to understand how this happened."

Haoyu spun in his chair, and his shoulders shrugged off her concern. "Your fabricator needs calibration."

Min shook her head. "Max checked. Diagnostics came back clean on our fabricator. She printed a new sample as well, which withstood quality testing. As did the casing on your bench."

His hand ran over his jet-black hair without a single strand moving. *He probably makes his own bespoke fixer,* she thought.

"And anyone can see," she pointed to the microscopy display, "that is an impact crater. A tiny, tiny impact crater."

"No way," he repeated. His tone was emphatic, but flat with boredom. "You have to be wrong. You girls haven't taken good care of your fabricator." He accented his patronizing words with another lazy shrug of his shoulder. The dismissive gesture smashed Min's frustration buttons.

"Haoyu, please," she begged. She hated the sound, wished her voice carried more confidence. "If it's the fabricator, help me verify it. That's all I'm asking."

He sniffed. "You know, there's a fantastic internal study on proper fabricator calibration for synthetic optics. Read it before-"

"I *wrote* that paper," she explained. The tone of her voice belied the roiling anger at being patronized yet again by her male counterpart.

Haoyu's smug face remained unperturbed at Min's expertise. "Regardless, I don't have to prove anything. This problem is on you and Max."

The open combativeness wasn't a shock from the Materials Engineer. Min took a moment to breathe, recalling the guidance Waffel had offered during her first year of graduate work: *Stay calm. When a man gets uncalm, he's seen as passionate. Strong. A leader or savior. When a woman does it, she's a bitch.*

Haoyu's hands rested behind his head, and he relaxed into the chair as his knees fell open. His eyebrows rose in a challenge.

Min inhaled a long breath of the lab's tepid air - after passing through the purification system, it took on a vague aroma of salted dough. It was an odor Min disliked. Max cherished it, claiming the smell was like the sculpting putty she made as a kid. As Min processed the sensation, she recalled Waffel's second piece of guidance: *The fastest way to a man's balls is through his ego.*

"Did I mention this failure occurred during a live demonstration to the Department of Defense?"

His brow collapsed as his eyes widened. "What was that?"

"The apparatus cracked during a funding demo." Not a lie. The demonstration worked, for a fraction of a second before something compromised the casing. "Waffel's got eighty million on the line for this project."

He didn't speak. In the silence, Haoyu swallowed.

"We need to explain to Waffel what failed. If you can find an issue in my fabrication, then she won't have to scrutinize the Modern Materials lab and its data."

The threat of impending bureaucracy got his attention. His legs closed, elbows landing on his knees as he leaned forward. "She'd order a full audit?"

Now it was Min's turn to shrug. "Wouldn't you if it meant that much funding?"

The man seemed to read something on the floor.

Min pushed her case. "How long did the last audit take?"

"Three weeks, plus overtime," he mumbled. "We got dick accomplished. Postponed our schedules by two months, all said and done."

"You have better stuff to do, don't you?" Min scooted her chair a few inches towards him, close enough to touch him. "So, which sounds less infuriating, eight weeks with nothing to show for it? Or a few hours of your time ending in proof of your flawless work?"

Her fingers brushed his knee, spinning him to the digital microscopy display.

Haoyu's gaunt cheeks puffed with a sigh. "Give me an hour to burn the casing off."

Over the next eighty minutes, Haoyu used a chemical laser to dissolve the polymer casing into two horizontal pieces. Min knew he was finished when the intense pulses of orange light stopped.

"Casing cut is clean," he reported. "Preparing to remove."

Min got close enough to share his view of the monitor. "Can you refocus over the point of impact?"

"Yep." Haoyu eased his finger over a touchpad, and the digital microscope moved. The screen followed the three-inch crack until a round hole came into frame. At this magnification, it might have been a stripmine - layers of depth torn from stratified material.

"Looks like it hit the lens," Min offered.

"Let's find out." His fingers shot into the control gloves that translated his hand movements to the robotic armatures and provided sensory feedback from the artificial digits. He flexed, and the delicate fingers of the armature respond with a mimicking motion, although at a far smaller scale. Pincers gripped the two ends of the casing and lifted.

Min's eyes shot to the monitor. Some kind of internal damage frosted the pristine artificial glass. "Can you remove the lens? Set it on its side?"

Haoyu did as she asked and refocused the microscope to encompass the entire lens. It was spider-webbed, a cone of fragmentation extending three-quarters of the way through the glass.

Min didn't speak, but pointed to the sharp tip of the destruction as Haoyu centered and increased magnification. Once. Twice. Then again.

"Definitely foreign matter in there," the materials engineer reported. Min saw it—a dark, tiny speck, even at this scale, yet obvious in the pristine clarity of the surrounding silica.

"What is that?"

"Not sure. Some kind of debris. I say we run it through the spectrometer and learn what it's made of. Should offer some clue."

Min bit back her smile at Haoyu's sudden proactive stance. "Sounds good to me."

Ten minutes later, the mass spectrometer was analyzing a vaporized sample of the pulverized glass. Haoyu had the molecular composition up on his display: 80% silicon, 10% carbon, 6% magnesium, and 4%

aluminum. Min recognized those components as the artificial lens material. Her stare flowed down the report to the list of trace elements.

One was listed: UNKNOWN (~128).

"What does that mean?" Min asked, turning to Haoyu. "There are 128 unknown trace elements?"

He shook his head, his tongue poking at the inside of his cheek. "No, no, it's one trace element. Something the machine doesn't recognize. That number is an estimate, but it's impossible."

"An estimate of what?"

"The trace element's atomic number," he clarified. "But, that's impossible, Minerva."

"You keep saying that."

"I mean it this time," he countered. His face was a mask of stress. "There's no way that's accurate. The heaviest element we have on the periodic table is Norrison, with an atomic weight of 120. This is an extra eight protons beyond anything humans have encountered or designed. Just not workable."

Min picked at her lip with the upper teeth for several seconds. "Ok, let's say for argument's sake that this is element 128. Would it crack your polymer?"

"It would have to be hauling ass," he said. "I would have to run simulations to be certain. My guess is it would need to be traveling at about 2% the speed of light. Again, not reasonable."

Min huffed. She loved science, but the stream of unknowns was exhausting. She came to Haoyu with one question: what broke my optics? Now, Min had the answer, along with more questions: where did this unknown element come from, and how did it achieve such an acceleration?

"Any holes in the walls of your lab?" Haoyu asked.

"Integrity sensors reported nothing, and they're accurate to a few nanometers."

Haoyu's gaze drifted, a shadow of his mind's search for excuses.

Min stood. "Do you know where this came from? Are you, or is anyone else, experimenting with new element creation? Is this from another lab at Daft?"

He stared through her, his eyes shifting as thoughts bounced behind them. "I don't think so, Min. Natural stellar forging is the only way I can conceive of creating this element."

"There's no way to manufacture element 128?"

He held up a palm. "If that's artificial, then whoever made it is decades ahead of Daft."

"Okay," she replied. Min licked the small tear she left on her lip. "Do me a solid, run the diagnostics on your spectrometer, then shoot another sample through, okay?"

"Sure. Should have the data tomorrow morning."

"Thanks." Min spun to leave the Modern Materials lab, intent on returning to the Foresight lab. Max was double-checking the walls for damage, and Min hoped she found some.

Haoyu called out before she got to the door. "One more thing."

She stopped and turned.

"If this sample came from a star, there's no way it's local."

"Local?" she asked.

"I mean, there's no evidence of this element existing in our solar system, Min. Our star isn't big enough to produce this element. This matter had to come from another star."

4

ABSTRACT SPIRAL

Min exited the Materials lab, her head heavy with questions. Words spun around the problems in her head as she walked the halls. Muscle memory guided her on the path to her lab, and her sneakers squeaked a familiar acoustic pattern on the floor. Waffel would demand an explanation, and right now, she couldn't offer one.

Well, you see Dr. Waffel, an extra-solar chunk of matter traveling about 12 million meters per second passed through our clean room during the key segment of your smoke and mirrors for the DoD. You know, these things happen.

Except they didn't. Science never happened that way. Even with the shitty quality control and reckless schedules the Daft Institute forced her to meet, this kind of super-random crap never occurred. The odds of it were indistinguishable from zero. There was another, simpler explanation. There had to be. A train of logic that wouldn't shred her doctorate before she received it. She had to find it before Waffel lost her mind.

Min's optimism eroded as she opened the door into the Foresight lab. The air tingled, pressurized with the calamity of a premium-tier Waffel tirade. At first, Min thought her advisor was screaming; however, a quick scan of the control room showed it was empty of people. Max was visible in the window, arms crossed across her chest, face clenched in a scowl. Max and their boss were in the clean room, and

Max must have left the comms channel open so she could listen to music as she picked apart the clean room for damage.

Waffel's voice came through the desk speakers, amplified to the insane level Max liked her music. "I don't care what it takes, Maxine. Just get it done! We have five days to come through or Daft tanks the project, along with your job at the Institute."

"Yes, I heard you the first three times you said that, Doctor. Saying it again doesn't magically make it possible." Max was pissed. The engineer wasn't adept at hiding her emotions. It didn't matter, as Waffel was void of empathy.

"Well, making it possible is the only reason you two are here," Waffel said. Min crossed the room until her advisor's flapping jowls appeared in the window. Her height wasn't much more than Max's, but she had three times the mass. "If you can't do that, you're of no use."

Min sighed. The women were flailing in a prideful spiral, and she considered how alike her advisor and her engineer were. Reliant on core convictions, albeit different ones. Min stepped to the window and knocked on the glass. With the comms open, the volume cranked to Max's enjoyment levels, the tap was downright percussive.

Max startled, and Waffel gasped. For a moment, their expressions conjured an image from childhood: Min's mother squirting the squabbling cats with a spray of water.

"I have news from the Modern Materials lab," she said. "Why don't you two come in here and let's talk?"

Sitting at her console, with Max and Waffel looking over her shoulders, Min pulled up the data from Haoyu's microscope on one of her screens. "There's evidence of an impact with the optics array. You can see it here. And we found some foreign debris embedded in the lens."

"Bullshit," Waffel exploded.

Min raised a calming hand. "I know it seems impossible. Haoyu thought so too. But when we zoom in," Min said as she flipped to the higher magnifications, "you can see it with your own eyes."

"What the hell is it? Where did it come from?" Max asked. "How did it-"

"It doesn't matter," Waffel said. "I'll deal with your shoddy clean room protocols after we get our funding."

Min's gaze left the screen and snapped to Waffel's face. She looked wrung-out. "How's that? Did the presentation-"

"We've got five days," Waffel interrupted again. "Five days until General Gates takes his entourage and money back to the Pentagon. As I was explaining to our engineer here, I salvaged your failed demo enough to get us a second chance."

"It didn't fail, though." Max's arms crossed over her chest. "We made it work even after you went-"

"Enough!" Waffel shouted. "Five days, ladies. Rebuild Foresight and prove your worth. Or I won't have funding to keep either of you on."

Min blanched, and felt the heat emanating from Max's explosive core. "Doctor, it'll take longer than that to print new optics."

"Then design the conventional components out of the system, Min. Remove the part that broke."

"I'm sorry?" Min was dumb-founded. Waffel was asking for the impossible. Optics were necessary to augment the limited amount of light that the aperture could manipulate. To magnify it to something visible. As they expand the ring to imprint more photons, the energy requirements would increase exponentially.

"I tried to explain it to her," Max said, her mind keeping pace with Min's. "She doesn't seem to get that we're already hitting the wall of the Institute's power system."

"Max is right, we can't-"

"You will." Waffel sighed, brushing her hands together as if dusting them off. "You'll figure it out. I have every confidence in you two." The woman moved to the lab's main door, ending the conversation by pulling herself out of it.

Min's jaw worked, but bafflement ate her words. As Waffel pulled open the door, she paused and spoke over her shoulder. "Five days. I'd get cracking if I were you."

The hiss and snap of the door's pneumatics ended the exchange. Min's mind raced, trying to link impossibilities together into a solution. Max unfolded herself and sank into her chair, one leg draping over the armrest while the other pivoted her on the chair's swivel. Min's gaze landed on the engineer, who stared with a solemn affect.

"Well," Min broke the artificial silence of the lab, "I'm open to ideas. My initial estimate is that we'll need about ten gigawatts of power to expand the aperture to three millimeters."

"Is that big enough to see anything without optics, Min?"

"I don't know," she replied. "It should be. I won't be sure until we try it, but we can't. We would need four more fission reactors at our disposal, or a capacitor field larger than the Daft campus to store that much power. Hell, the cabling to carry the energy into the ring is impractical to make." The conundrums were stacking, and Min felt the dirty nails of apprehension scratch the inside of her ribs.

"We need power," Max stated. Her swivel has turned to a 360 degree spin. Where anxiety locked Min up, it gave Max the wiggles. Min watched her friend twirl, the repetition and gliding motions calming. Then Max paused, pressing her foot on the floor to stop the chair's movement. The back of her head tilted down, and Min followed her gaze to the dog bed.

"What is it?" Min probed.

A languid sigh escaped the engineer as her hands wiped across her cheeks. Min couldn't see her face, but knew the motions well: Max was crying.

"Max, it's okay. We'll figure something out. And even if we don't, we'll have our choice of jobs, right?"

"It's not that," she replied. Her voice carried a tremor. "I might know someone who can help. Someone who owes me one hell of a favor."

5

Good Goose

Max split the next twelve hours between prepping the clean room for a new build and collapsing out of consciousness in the fold-out cot behind her desk. Min had started fabrication on the pair of larger apertures about eight hours ago, but it would take a while to weave in the coil of vanadium dioxide that enabled them to do their weird magic. The time was a gift. She used it to steel her nerves about her task.

Power Systems occupied the two floors beneath her lab. The upper floor housed an array of supercapacitors - the same ones they used to drive the demo for Waffel's shitty presentation. The Power System labs filled the lower floor, where Max was trudging now.

The doors were pale white insets in the pale white walls that framed the pale white polymer that never seemed to get dirty. The only clue to what lay beyond etched in the onyx glass plate set at eye-level.

The placard in front of her read: POWER SYSTEMS - RESEARCH AND DEVELOPMENT.

Months of dreading this moment clumped in her throat. Max swallowed it down, whipped up her resolve, and opened the door.

Every Daft lab followed a similar design. One main entry leading to a common space, where anyone could enter without clearance. The Institute's philosophy that "Science Abhors Silos" had been plastered on motivational posters in the cafeteria. Of course, that attitude carried only so far: innovation required security, so common areas branched off into places accessible only by those assigned to them. In her tiny lab, the clean room was their only secure area. With Power Systems being such a large group, there were dozens of these protected segments branching off their common space: clean rooms, storage and materials, data warehousing, engineering workbenches, and so forth.

The Power Systems common room was a cube farm. A few open areas housed conference tables and chairs, and Daft's official shade of not-quite-white blanched every surface. She could spend hours exploring the common room before finding who she needed. Max didn't have hours.

She hoisted herself onto a chair, peering over the walls of the farm. Max cupped her hands around her mouth and hollered, "Goose?"

A few heads prairie-dogged: gape-mouthed nerds poking out of their cubicles to assess the danger. After a second or two, they skulked back into their secure work-nests. All except for one.

Max traced the path from her current location to Bruce, memorizing the turns and counts through the cube maze. She stepped off the stool and made her way towards Dr. Gose's bullpen.

He was still standing when Max rounded the final partition. Bruce was tall; most people seemed big to Max, but Bruce's height surpassed the average person. An icy blue stare pierced his glasses, the lenses so thick they compressed the shape of the man's thin face and making his pupils appear too-close-together. His mouth was unreadable, hidden by a scruffy blond beard, but from the way his facial hair was moving, she could tell he was chewing on the inside of his cheek.

"Max. Couldn't stay away?"

She bit her tongue, taking a breath before she cussed him out.

Bruce continued before she could speak. "I've been meaning to head upstairs. Express my condolences. And appreciation." He sniffled through his bristles.

Max shrugged. She hadn't spoken to Bruce since the accident two months ago; in fact, she'd been avoiding him. She was not ready to have this conversation, yet she needed to. "Listen, I don't want to be here, okay? But my lab needs some help and I think you're the guy."

Bruce Gose—dubbed "Bruce Goose" by his colleagues, although Max seemed to be the only person who would say it in front of the man—blinked behind his glasses. His chewing stopped, and he swallowed something. "I suppose I owe you."

"Can we chat in private?"

A minute later, they were in Bruce's engineering workspace. Larger than the Foresight clean room, filled with shelves of components and worktops cluttered with half-finished assemblies and control boards. Bruce mounted his stool, feet slapping the lower support bar. His finger found the level beneath the seat, and he raised the height until he was just-above-eye-level with Max.

"What do you need?" he asked.

Max had trouble looking at him. The anger was still there, percolating in her gut. This man killed her dog. Perhaps not directly, but he bore responsibility for it. Max knew it, and so did Bruce. Her gaze wandered over the closest surface.

"Earlier this year, you mentioned you were working on a monster power source. Something small and simple, but capable of massive output. Is that true?"

The man's expression brightened as the conversation turn towards his work. "You mean this?" His stool rumbled against the floor as he swung to the bench behind him. He grabbed what appeared to be a metal water bottle - the kind folks carry and reuse to reduce plastic waste. It looked hefty in his hands, though, as if it carried ten times its volume of liquid.

Max nodded. "Is that one of the..." She couldn't recall the name of the project.

"Power bottle," Bruce offered. "Yep, this is the latest prototype."

"Explain to me again how it works," she said. Her arms relaxed from their defensive hold across her ribs.

"It's pretty amazing. It's a magnetic containment structure for an artificial singularity. The radiation released is focused by the magnetic field and emitted as power."

Max surveyed the container with skepticism. "So, there's an actual black hole in there?"

Bruce smiled and puffed his chest, impressed with himself.

"Is it safe?"

Bruce answered by lobbing the bottle in an arc towards Max. Her hands shot from her sides and tried to catch the thing, but missed. It clanked on the floor tiles, bouncing across the workspace and ricocheting against the far wall.

"Bruce!" Max scolded. Her cheeks flushed with panic.

He chuckled, "Don't worry. Yes, it's safe. Near indestructible. If you cracked it, you'd have to breach the magnetic containment inside for the singularity to escape. Even then, the black hole is so small it would evaporate in a second or two."

Max walked over to the bottle and picked it up. It was weightier than it looked, but easy to lift. The iridescent blue metal formed a cylinder, about twenty centimeters long and fifteen in diameter. One end was flat, the other tapered down to a circular opening that Max recognized. It was the standard power coupling used at the Institute.

"So you just hook this up, and electricity comes out?" she asked.

"Well, actually no," Bruce started. "I mean yeah, it links in like any other power source we have here. But unless you feed the black hole, it'll evaporate as you pull energy. Eventually it would disappear."

"Feed it?"

"Matter becomes radiation. It goes in, energy comes out."

Max rolled the thing from hand to hand.

"How do I do that?" she asked. When Bruce didn't answer, she lifted her gaze to him. His hooded eyes probed her as a parent tries to understand the actions of their toddler.

"What are you up to, Max?" he finally asked.

6

Power Move

Max leaned against the workbench and shrugged. "We need a super-duper power source. You have one. We're going to use it."

Bruce closed his eyes, easing his head back and forth. "I'm sorry, but I can't let you take this. I'd love to, but..."

"Bruce-"

"It's not my choice. Waffel will cut my dick off. The power bottle is beyond Top Secret. You even knowing about it could get me reprimanded. Letting you use it will end my employable status."

Max locked stares with him, keeping her face inscrutable and letting the man's career anxiety wrestle his survivor's guilt.

"Max, I mean it."

She held his gaze in silence, feeling the cool metal in her fingers.

"There's no way-"

"Okay," Max said. "Fine. We'll figure something else out." She rotated the bottle, pretending to examine it further. "I doubt it could generate the level of power we need, anyway."

Bruce stiffened. "How much are you looking for?"

Max held back her smile as her hook sank into Bruce's ego. "Ten gigawatts, sustained."

Bruce relaxed into himself, waved a derisive hand at her.

"Why? How much can the bottle produce?"

He snorted, pushing his eyeglasses higher on his narrow nose. "We haven't hit the limit yet. The last test sequence we pulled a consistent 94 gigawatts for almost two minutes before the singularity dispersed."

Max couldn't hold her jaw closed. That rivaled the output of 50 nuclear power plants. And she was holding it in one hand.

A smug grin reshaped his stupid beard. "And that's bench testing. On paper, the power is infinite. In practice?" He shrugged. "We're close to a working Hawking regulator that should prolong evaporation by a factor of years." He pulled off his glasses, cleaning them on the hem of his white lab coat before popping them back onto his face. "Just one bottle that size could provide enough power for the world for centuries. Effective, clean, perpetual energy, Max."

Her heart fluttered at the thought of it. No more resource conflicts or trade wars for energy. Humanity could work together on real and bigger problems.

"Which is why Waffel and the Institute don't want anyone knowing about it. The market cap on this project is incalculable." Bruce clucked. "You're holding the power commodity of the future. Daft will own the market."

Her reverie seethed into a pool of disgust. Of course Daft would focus on revenue and profit. Not people.

Bruce stood, wiping his lab coat flat before his fingers lifted the bottle out of her hand. "You'll have to wait until the project gets reclassified and made available inside of the Institute, just like everyone else, Max."

He placed the bottle on the workbench. Max's gaze ascended from the bottle to his weary and apologetic face.

"I saved your life, Bruce."

He nodded. "I know. And I know what it cost you. And I am forever in your debt."

"That dog was everything to me. You *owe* me."

He nodded again. "I appreciate you loved Neils Bork - hell, we all loved that dog. And if you wanted anything else, I'd oblige. The bottle is a no-go, Max." He moved aside her and opened the workspace door, letting in the low rabble from the common area. Then gestured with a hand, asking her to leave without a word.

Max eyed the iridescent device on the workbench, crossing her arms as she stomped past him. She continued straight along the wall, heading to the exit instead of Bruce's bullpen.

"Max," he called after her.

She quickened her pace, nerves fraying. She clutched herself tighter.

"C'mon, we can figure-"

She yanked the door open, smashing the doorstop with a *thump* that she was sure caused several more heads to pop up from their hidey-holes. She ignored Bruce's pleas for understanding, those words fading into the sound of her squeaking boots as she raced to the stairs. The growing burn in her legs distracted from her anger.

Neils Bork had been her best friend. Her familiar and her rock. Always gentle and kind with fuzzy nuzzles, ready to brighten the day with play. He had been the adopted mascot for the lab. Everyone who knew him loved him. The pain of those last moments returned as she arrived at her floor. Tears welled in her eyes, and she bee-lined for her lab at the end of the hallway.

They had been out for their morning walk around campus, and had stopped at the bakery for some bagels. As Bork led the return route to the Institute's research center, Bruce crossed their path. Unoffensive chit-chat ensued, and Bruce started blathering about his work. Stuff Max didn't grasp, more science fiction to her than science. Bruce got on a roll about gravity well depth and ionizing radiation, and he stopped reading his environment.

In his self-indulgent pontification, Bruce failed to clock the speeding truck as he walked onto Lovelace Avenue. The snap decision came down on Max. In one arm she carried a sack full of bagels and schmear, and in the other she gripped Bork's leash. In that moment of panic, she dropped the lead to grab Bruce's shirt and yank him out of harm's way.

She saved Bruce. She protected the food. And she lost Neils Bork.

In her own space now, Max dropped into her chair. Her weeping gaze fell to the empty dog bed - the one she couldn't bring herself to get rid of. Where Bork should lie today. His intelligent umber stare on her, his adoration bottomless as his tail beat the floor like it owed him money. Ready for a walk; for cuddles; for whatever Max needed. But now this lab was silent, calm, and hollow.

She took a controlled breath. Willed her chest to relax as her arms unwrapped from her torso. Sweat slicked her stomach, her body heat amplified by her stifling over-sized sweater.

Her right hand extended from its loose sleeve, holding the power bottle she swiped from Bruce's workshop. In the brighter light of the Foresight lab, the container's surface shimmered. What appeared as an oily iridescence in Bruce's dank workshop she now realized was more proactive. The bottle's surface glowing from some organic inner state, as if it reflected the mood of the singularity inside.

She slipped off the crushing wool sweater and wiped her tears on its cuff. Max whispered, "Like I said, Bruce. You owe me."

7

HAIL MARY

The previous apertures appeared as little more than boogers of solder gobbed on a circuit board; not big enough to detect the hole in the ring's center without a micrometer laser. The new one looked like a ring. A tiny circle mounted upright on the silicon wafer, the only circuitry being two leads, ending at a standard power coupling. Max held it up to the ceiling LEDs and saw the pinprick of white light through the ring's center.

"You sure that aperture is large enough?" Max asked. "Will the camera see anything?"

"Mathematically, yes. This is the same diameter as the light output from the old optics assembly." Min's voice was distant. Max glanced down to find Min scrutinizing the power bottle. Her fingers held it by the tapered end, her arm extended as far as possible. "And this thing is safe?"

"Bruce says it is."

"And you're sure this can deliver the juice we need?"

"It will. Unless Bruce is making shit up to fluff his ego. We'll know soon enough."

Min looked to her friend, and the women shrugged as they exchanged components. Max watched her align the new ring into the path of the laser, placing the PCB ahead of the stream of light exiting the quartz crystal. She knelt down, sighting the beam into the aperture until the green dot appeared on the wall. In the past, this alignment required an hour of careful calibration using delicate servos to position the circuit board on the workbench. An offset of microns would cause the laser to miss the opening altogether. With the larger aperture, accuracy had become less of a concern.

Once Min mounted the PCB, Max decoupled the Foresight telescope from the Institute's power grid and wired in the bottle. It left her underwhelmed: this setup was too simple to work. No nuclear reactor behind meters of concrete and lead feeding an immense matrix of barrel capacitors connected to tons of cabling that fed into her lab. Instead, there was a single connector on which she twisted the bottle's lip until the safety prongs snapped closed. She set the bottle on the floor and traced the braided cables to the power splitter installed under the workbench. From there, the circuitry remained the same as before. Power ran to two gateways: one powered the laser emitter, and the other the aperture.

Max stood, arched her back to stretch the kink in her left hip. The straining muscle carried in her voice. "This works, and we could pack the entire telescope in a laptop bag, power and all."

Min ran a hand over her hair, pulling it into the ponytail already there. Her eyes narrowed with skepticism. "*If* this works. This feels like a Hail Mary."

Max sniffed and released a long sigh of relief as she relaxed her pose. "Is that a... a sports thing?"

"It is," Min responded as her hand left her head and found her lab coat pocket. "Are we ready? It feels like we shouldn't be ready. It should have been more difficult to set up."

"I'd say we're ready for step one. Let's power each circuit incrementally. See if Bruce is full of shit before we run a complete test."

Min moved to the control room door. She pushed it open, and the women rounded the desk to take their respective seats. Their movements became reflex as they entered a pattern. Headsets landing over their ears; microphone lowering to their lips; a quick comms test; status check of telemetry feeds from the clean room. It was all familiar until they reached the last system component: power.

At the point Min would query the capacitor levels they paused with uncertainty. Max peeled her eyes from her screen to find Min's face turned to her. The display behind Min carried live camera feeds: half the display monitoring individual components of Foresight, and the image from the telescope output on the other.

Min shrugged. "I guess... I guess we can't verify power readiness." A statement and a question.

Knowing Min, she was offering Max a last chance to back out of this test. Smiling back at the physicist, Max replied, "Guess not. We'll read the power flow after opening the main coupling."

Min nodded and spun her chair back to her terminal. "Okay, let's crack open that bottle."

Max faced her console and issued the command. "Coupler is open. Reading..." Her heart fell. "Reading zero watts."

Min's reply was quick, "I think that's okay. Didn't you say it only emits power when there was a demand?"

"I believe Bruce said that, yes. What are you thinking?"

"Open the circuit to the emitter. That should pull a few hundred milliwatts."

"Got it," Max replied. "Powering the laser." She issued new commands via her console, opening the pathway between the splitter and the laser. Her instrumentation responded as red warning lights painted the observation window. "Showing a steady flow of 312 milliwatts."

The flurry of relief in her chest warbled her voice, with her words coming out close to laughter.

She checked on Min. Her lab partner's stare remained locked on the images on her screen. "How's it looking?"

"As good as ever," Min replied. "This is very encouraging."

She glanced back at her dashboard. Max had to agree. "Power levels are stable." The lilt in her tone betrayed her surprise: maybe Bruce wasn't just swinging his dick about his black-hole-in-a-bottle. "I'm ready to power the aperture if you are."

The sigh from Min was calming, or hesitant. Max was uncertain. "Okay, fire it up," she said. "Start with what we've seen work. Feed it one gigawatt."

This was the proper test. Could the bottle produce enough energy?

"Drawing one gigawatt." Max typed the command. Her jaw dropped at the instrumentation changes. When using the supercapacitor array, the ramp-up in power took milliseconds. There were concrete reasons for this: variability in the efficiency of individual barrel capacitors or their distance from the aperture caused delays for the energy to arrive. But this transfer was reported as instant. "Steady at one gigawatt. Holy shit, the envelope was immediate! Power just... showed up!"

"The apparatus looks good, too," Min replied. "Laser is showing some modulation." Without the second ring, there was no source of information to imprint, resulting in random changes in the entangled beam. "Open the feed to two gigs, Max."

The telemetry remained steady. "Two gigawatts confirmed. I'm not seeing any measurable fluctuations in power output." Another anomaly that left her dumbfounded: while the capacitors provided a stable emission of power, the levels *always* wobbled. Not enough to matter, but sufficient for the instrumentation to detect. The bottle emitted energy at a precision she couldn't measure. "We're okay to increase power on your call."

Another exhale came from Min, the trepidation it carried amplified in Max's headset. "Go to three gigawatts, then." Max filled her lungs, too, recognizing the musky odor of the empty dog bed at her feet.

They repeated the sequence twice, breaching five gigawatts. More than twice the power they'd ever consumed. Half of what they needed. Every measurement held pristine. The telemetry was so steady, the only verification that Max's screen hadn't frozen was the timer incrementing in the upper-left corner.

"Min, we're good to shut down. Everything says the bottle works as advertised. I'm not sure how long it can sustain this output without evaporating. I don't think Bruce will give us another one."

Silence. Max repeated the request to kill the power test, spinning her chair to face her colleague.

Min stared at her monitor. Leaned in close, as if each pixel hid a thousand more.

"What's up?" Max asked. Her friend was ignoring her, but her posture didn't convey something was wrong; instead, Min's lean into her monitor suggested a sense of rapture. "Minerva Draper's brain, please report to the Foresight control room," she jabbed.

Her friend still didn't respond.

Max's nerves prickled with worry. "Min, what is it?"

Min placed a finger on the screen and faced her. "Does this look random to you?"

Max's gaze flitted up Min's arm to the screen displaying the digital camera tracking the output of the laser. The figure there was low-fidelity, but coherent.

The lime light bent into drab silhouetted shapes: a broad cylinder on the bottom of the image, with a cone shape on top. As she watched, details emerged in the pale light. Contours formed. The shape moved in a coordinated and organic motion that tugged a thread in her memory. One woven into recent events, lashed to her emotional well-being.

Not random at all. In fact, Max recognized it. Her brain was filling in missing detail of course, yet she was certain. As if responding to her stare, the shape on the screen shifted. The cone elongated, seemed to revolve over the cylinder twice before easing down onto it.

Her lip trembled, and she scooted closer. Not believing. Wanting to deny the visage she had seen daily for years. The habit of her friend preparing his pillowy bed next to her desk for a snooze.

"That's not random," she whispered. "It's my dog, laying down for a nap."

8

PASS THE BOTTLE

"There's no way," Min repeated. "Neils Bork died over two months ago."

"I am aware of that," Max snapped, placing a finger on the repeating video of the green blobs she believed were her dead dog. "But I also know that dog like my heartbeat, and that is him!"

Min sighed, holding her tongue while Max doubled-down on her sentimental argument. When Bork died, she had prompted the engineer to take time off, process her loss, sort her guilt and anger. Instead, Max worked more. Spent longer days and more overnights in the lab. And now a backflow of unprocessed emotions was blowing up in their faces.

Min reasserted logic into the debate. "We don't even have another aperture, Max. That means there's no data stream to imprint on the laser, right?"

Max's curls bounced as she wagged her head. "You're the one who said the image isn't random, not me. You recognized a pattern to it."

Min's tongue pressed into the back of her teeth. "I think I said it was 'anomalous-'"

"You said it 'wasn't random,' Min. Those images are not random data."

"Okay, but isn't it more likely to be something simple? Light noise. Refraction off the lip of the aperture, hitting the camera. A lens aberration-"

"There are no lenses!" Max stressed. "We removed them all, remember?"

Shit. Max was right about the lenses. "Of course, but-"

"And we can measure noise, rule it out?"

"Yes, and we will, but-"

Max's mouth jerked open, and Min raised a finger. "Please, listen. I appreciate you miss your dog, okay? I do too." Max's lips pressed together. Her smoky eye makeup amplified the sudden grief hitting her eyes, white pools glistening in a field of sallow gray. Min continued, "Neils Bork is gone, though. Even if that image isn't some error factor, how could it be Bork?"

Max's gaze wobbled, then fell to her own boots. Her small hands gripped the top of her thighs, and Min leaned close to take those hands in her own. "It's okay, Max. Whatever you're feeling right now isn't right or wrong. It just *is.* "

Min felt a warm tear hit her thumb, and she moved to hug her friend.

"I want him back." Max's voice was a diminutive squeak, with a warble so pronounced Min had trouble deciphering the words. "I miss him so much."

"Me too, Max. He was a wonderful dog. The best."

Min held her for a minute, letting the woman sob into the shoulder of her coat. This was the first unconstrained expression of grief Max had shared over Neils Bork. It wouldn't be the last. The tender moment ended when the door to their lab shot open.

"Where the hell is it?" Dr. Gose whisper-screamed. The shock of his arrival caused Max's head to bounce up in surprise, bumping Min on the cheek.

Min spun to face him, scooting her chair in front of Max to let the engineer collect herself. "What's wrong, Bruce? Where's the fire?"

Bruce glared at her, then pivoted to watch the Foresight lab door ease closed on its pneumatics. With the clap of the latch catching, he returned his antagonizing stare to the women. "You comprehend that you're fucking with the most destructive force in the universe, right?"

Min shook her head, not following.

"Where the fuck is my bottle, Max? The one from my workshop?" With the door closed, the lab in full sound-absorption, Bruce screamed. "Do you realize the trouble I'm in?"

It took a second of brow-wrinkling before Min understood. She heaved out a sigh. "You weren't aware Max borrowed the bottle."

Bruce jutted forward two steps, jabbing the air with a finger. "*Borrow?* No, that bitch stole it!"

"Watch your mouth, Doctor!" Min stood and closed the distance to Bruce. She batted the man's indignant hand away. "I'm happy to sort this out, but I won't have you spit misogyny in my lab!"

The man paled, seemed to shrink an inch below Min's height. "Look," he said, his tone controlled if not cordial, "I see your current pickle, but if Waffel finds that bottle here, or realizes it's missing from Power Systems R&D, that's it for me. No job. Federal prison would be on the table. You understand?"

Min held up a hand as if pausing Bruce, then turned to Max. The engineer's eyes were puffy, yet her makeup somehow unperturbed from crying as she met Min's questioning stare. After a few breaths, she spoke. "I was going to return it."

Min wilted, a bitter tang rising into her mouth. "Max? Why?"

"We need it, Min. Waffel gave us impossible parameters. I was only fulfilling them." Her shadowy gaze flitted past Min to the man behind her. "Bruce had the answer, and he owes me."

From behind her, Min heard Bruce gulp his guilt. She returned her gaze to him and lowered her hand. "I'm sorry, Dr. Gose. Max will remove the bottle-"

"Min, no!"

She shushed Max's protest before continuing, "She will disconnect the bottle and you can take it with you. We're not looking to cause you trouble. Okay?"

The man stared, and his face softened as if the red of his anger faded to reveal Max's distress. "Dammit," he huffed.

"What?" Min asked.

The man's posture melted, and his hands found his lab coat pocket. He looked between them before speaking—a parent preparing to admonish their children. "You two realize the consequences, correct? You get that if you let the singularity feed too much, it'll breach the bottle? And then consume whatever matter is around? Like the fucking planet? You understand that, right?"

Min nodded, looking at Max. Max shrugged, which Min read to mean she was also unsure where Bruce was heading. She turned back to Dr. Gose. "We're aware of how singularities work."

"And that if you pull too much power, the singularity will evaporate? And it'll cost Daft just short of a billion dollars to create another one?"

Now Min blanched. *A billion? With a 'b'?* The cost of the entire Foresight project since its inception didn't amount to a tenth of that. She looked through the window to the opalescent bottle resting under the Foresight telescope. That one container was more valuable than anything she might ever conceive.

Bruce's heaving sigh brought Min into the moment. "At least let me set you up with a Hawking regulator. Lower your chances of all of us finding out what infinite gravity feels like. Okay?"

Min looked at Max; her wide eyes and slack jaw mimicked the surprise Min was experiencing. They both turned to Bruce.

He rubbed his thinning hair with one hand, the other massaging his temple while his eyes clamped shut.

"You're letting us use the bottle?" Min asked.

His hands slapped to his sides, eyes popped open as if letting out the bad thoughts. "I've got a lab inventory in two days. I need everything back before then, or Waffel ruins us all."

The women stayed silent, afraid any squeak might chase away their fortune.

"And in that event," Bruce continued, his gaze falling to meeting Min's, "I think I'd prefer to get crushed in a black hole."

9

OCCHAM'S FAVOR

An hour later, Bruce returned to the Foresight lab with a small box—not the flat kind folks at the Institute carried around printed reports in, but the two-handed kind used for physical artifacts. He handed the box to Max and motioned toward their clean room. "I'll need to show you how this works."

Leading the way, Max opened the box. Inside, she found two familiar objects: another power bottle and a splitter. This bottle was more bulb-shaped, with no luster on its surface. The splitter was bulkier than the ones she used. "You replacing our bottle?" she asked.

"No," he replied as he closed the clean room door. "No, I'm augmenting it."

"You're adding a second power bottle? As in, why fuck with one black hole when two are twice as dangerous?"

"And twice as expensive," Bruce added. "But no, the bulb doesn't house another black hole." He tapped her shoulder and motioned for the box.

Max handed it over. "Okay. Explain."

Bruce squatted to the floor next to the Foresight workbench, and Max lowered herself to watch his work. Bruce set the box on the floor, then sent his long hands beneath the table to disconnect the stolen power bottle from the Foresight power circuit. The rough way he handled this equipment, with abundant confidence and disregard for physical jarring, made Max wonder if the man was bloating his ego by overstating the danger.

"Your black hole is feeding itself," he said. He held up the disconnected bottle, pointing a calloused fingertip at the shimmer crawling along the metal. "As it emits Hawking radiation, the magnetic containment forces those ions towards the singularity. The consumption creates a tiny amount of x-rays, which generate this 'aura' you see on the bottle."

"The x-rays aren't dangerous?"

A glib smile. Bruce had expected the question. "Not remotely. Haoyu created a material that absorbs it, transduces it to these photonic emissions." He stopped to stare at the phosphorescent display oozing across the metal. "It's downright trippy."

He set the bottle down, slid the box closer, and grabbed the bulb. "This is for overflow. The magnetic field in this one is shaped to contain the Hawking radiation. Store it for future use."

"Like a capacitor," Max said, seeking a mental connection to something familiar.

"In function, at least." His empty hand snatched the power coupling from the box, and with similar agile motions as before, he popped it onto the bulb with a quick twist. "This little doo-dad here," he tapped the coupler, "maintains the balance of radiation around the singularity. As you draw power, the radiation is used to power whatever is connected to the bottle. That starves the singularity, and it evaporates."

Max nodded, following the layperson's explanation. "And when you stop the draw, the radiation moves to this bulb?"

Bruce grinned, his yellowing teeth apparent under his facial hair in the harsh LED lighting. "Yep! If the regulator doesn't detect a draw of power, it shuttles the Hawking radiation into the bulb. If it detects too much evaporation in the singularity, it feeds it using radiation stored in the bulb. Here, watch this..."

He took the power bottle up in his free hand and snapped it home into the regulator. He held the contraption up, letting Max regard the ebbing shimmer on the bottle. Max found the fading glow both comforting and distressing.

"How can you tell if the black hole..." she searched for the term she needed, and didn't find it. "How do you know the singularity hasn't evaporated?"

Bruce pulled a pen from his lab coat pocket, using it to point out the glass tube set into the regulator's surface. "Notice that little bubble in there? That's a small bit of hydrogen," he explained. "It's suspended in a non-reactive oil, but see how it wobbles? That means radiation is passing through the regulator."

Max squinted, noting the subtle shift in the bubble's shape. "Why use something analog like that? Why not a digital sensor?"

Bruce's face fell, his lips retracting into his beard with disappointment. He reached under the table, flailing for the coupling a few times before finding it and connecting the new power source. "We use digital instrumentation, Max. But this looks cool."

Max smirked, but the squawk of the comms system belayed her sardonic reply. "If you're done, come to the control room. I have some questions for Bruce." It was Min, back from the fabricators with the second ring they needed for the DoD demo.

Max hopped to her feet, offered Bruce a hand as he struggled off his knees. He waved her off, but handed her the box to carry while he rose on wobbly legs. In the control room, Max found Min pushing a hand cart around their shared desk. On the dolly's large flat surface squatted a canvas bundle the size of a beach ball.

"What the heck is that?" Max asked. "I thought you went to fabricate our second aperture."

Min stopped pushing and caught her breath. Whatever it was, it was heavy for its size. Max reached out to touch it, pull back the tarp, but Min smacked her hand away.

"Don't! It's a surprise," she scolded, her eyes shooting darts at Max. "Are you two done in there?"

Max started to speak, but Bruce spoke over her. "You're good to go, should have more power than you'll ever need."

Min smiled and her eyes softened. "Awesome, thank you Bruce. We'll return it all in a couple of days."

"Two days," he emphasized. "If I don't have this in my lab by Wednesday morning, I'm raising Cain." He slid between the bulky hand truck and their desk. "Or more to the point, Waffel will. None of us want that."

Min nodded, an exaggerated movement that pulled her short hairs loose from her ponytail. Something was amiss, but Max knew to keep quiet while Bruce was there.

As he approached the door, he called over his shoulder. "We haven't run a field test with those new regulators yet. In fact," he stopped to turn around, "I'd appreciate any instrumentation you get from it, Max. It's the least you could do for me."

"Of course," Max said. "Least I could do."

Bruce's eyes flitted between the two women, and his mouth fell into a dour smirk. "Two days. Try not to kill us all." He turned and opened the door, and the soundscape in the lab expanded: the clop of steps in the hallway; the murmur of low-key conversations between people she couldn't see. Then the door closed in his wake, leaving the women in silence.

Max motioned to the canvas blob on the truck. "Do I want to know what that is?" Her gaze rose to find Min's lips tight and her cheeks reddening. Max recognized the look: her friend was nervous. "What'd you do, Min?"

10

Δ Problem of Units

"I fucked up, Max." Min sucked on her lips to hide their tremble.

The engineer's smoky gaze narrowed. "Is there a body? Do we need to rent a van?"

"No," Min said. Max's dark humor was not sitting well over her anxiety. "Nothing like that. I just..." She closed her eyes and bit her lip again. "I made a mistake at the fabricator."

Min opened her eyes to see Max gaping at the hand truck. "What kind of mistake?"

"A units error."

"What does that mean?"

"Um..." A tingle of stress tickled her sinuses. "I consumed several million dollars in materials."

Max's stare locked onto hers. "Oh shit, Min." She pointed at the canvas. "Is that... is that supposed to be our second three millimeter aperture?"

Min nodded, unable to stop the brimming tears on her cheeks. "Yep."

"But it's..." Max held up her hands, gesturing the way Min's father used to brag about the size of the fish he caught from the lake.

"It's three decimeters. Not millimeters."

Max's hands eased over her mouth as her brain calculated the amount of materials needed to create a ring this size.

"I used up our lab's quota of exotic metal for the next year, because I set the fabricator to the wrong units."

The engineer evaluated the hand truck as if it carried explosives. Min wanted her to speak. Say that it was okay. They could re-purpose the excessive aperture, or recycle it into smaller ones. But Max stood silent.

Min filled the silence with nervous chatter. "I guess I'm more exhausted than I realize, and you know how the fabricators have an auto-scaling option, right? I mean, who the hell works in decimeters anyway, Max? Why is that even an option?"

Max nodded, her pitying gaze rising to Min as her lips pulled into a worry. But she said nothing.

"And how could this happen? I mean, why aren't there protocols in place to prevent using this much material, Max?"

The engineer continued to bob her head as she moved to take Min into a hug. "You're right, Min. There should be safeguards. I'd bet money they're coming, once Waffel gets wind of this."

Quiet cries turned to sobs at the mention of her advisor and boss.

"Hey, if it's any consolation, they'll name the new protocols after you." Max's hands moved across her back in gentle reassurance. "Maybe your name will become a verb."

"What do you mean?"

"Oh, you know, as in, 'Hey, make sure you adhere to the Draper protocol. We don't want to Minerva this build.'"

The playful poke squeaked a laugh out of her, to Min's surprise and appreciation.

Max pulled away, adding, "Not the mark you intend to leave at the Daft Institute, but a mark nonetheless." Her thin fingers wiped the wetness from Min's face. "*Blech*. Good thing you never wear makeup."

"That way, I'm always ready to fail," Min said.

A sharp zing shot from her biceps as Max pinched playfully. "Stop with the self-deprecation, dammit. You made a mistake anyone else could have made, Min."

She appreciated the sentiment and empathy, but Min wasn't sure if she believed it. "Thanks, Max."

"Haven't I told you about Bruce's keyboard fiasco? Instead of creating one of those stupid custom keyboards he uses, he started a job printing thousands of them."

Min knew the story. Similar mistake, at a fraction of the cost.

"And the asshole called me at two in the morning when he couldn't cancel the print run. Everyone does this kind of crap, Min."

"Yeah, but-"

"Yes, this is going to be expensive, no doubt about it. We can hope it will prod the Institute to add some governance over the fabricators. Guard rails that should have been there to prevent this from happening."

Min shrugged, lost for feelings or words. Max was right. This over-scaled fabrication should have been impossible. But why was Min the one to prove it wasn't? Nobody chastised or reprimanded Bruce for his error. She was sure of that. Her anxiety bloomed from the hard conversation she'd have with Waffel and her superiors. And anger from the knowledge that Bruce or Haoyu would receive different treatment if they had taken the same actions. She shook the idea out of her skull, knowing it would end in a pity-party.

"We need another three millimeter aperture, though. I used all of our exotics quota to make this," Min looked down to the canvas tarp concealing her fifty kilogram error.

"Don't worry," Max said. She patted Min on the shoulder before moving to the push rail of the hand truck. "The quotas are just data. Guidelines. There's always slush factored in."

"Slush?" Min asked.

Max heaved her frame against the railing, her boots snickering on the tile floor before catching. "Yeah," she grunted. "It's not like the Institute doesn't have more material, right? Get the door for me?"

Min moved to the clean room entrance and pulled the door open. "What are you doing with it?"

Max caught her stride, and the heavy load gained momentum. She pivoted the rail-end around to fit everything through the door. "Moving it into the clean room, dumbass. If... or *when* Waffel comes screaming, don't you want this to appear intentional?"

"Intentional?" Min followed a few steps into the room, and Max settled the truck alongside the workbench.

"Yeah," she huffed, rising with her hands on her hips. "Who can say this wasn't part of our plan all along? We should make it look that way before Waffel loses her mind."

· • • ● ●· ● • • ·

It took hours to reconfigure the clean room for the new ring. During that time, Max scanned the huge aperture and designed a footing that could hold the heavy coil upright on the small workbench. Printed, the oblong brace looked like a massive hot dog bun, resulting in several crass jokes at Bruce's expense. The levity returning to the room calmed her, their shared sense of humor a comfort.

Once the new assembly was complete, Min watched through the window while Max reconnected the power.

"We'll need a bigger laser," Min said. The comms system was open between the control room and the clean room; Min's voice was being projected so Max could hear. "The giant aperture makes everything else so..." She shrugged, looking for the right word. "... puny."

Max's snort came through the desk speakers behind her. "Never expected you to have insecurities regarding size, Min. Guess Bruce is rubbing off on you."

Min chuckled. Her cheeks already hurt from laughing and crying over her million-dollar blunder. She gave silent thanks for Max and her pragmatic sense of humor.

"That does it," Max reported. "All wired up. Do you want to do one last alignment check?"

Threading a laser through a sub-millimeter gap mandated precision. Any jostle or breeze had the potential to cause the light to shift. If the beam didn't pierce the ring, the photons wouldn't react to the exotic metal's quantum manipulation properties, causing the entangled light to go unaffected. With an aperture this large, proper alignment was almost a given.

"No, not for the power-up test. Can you check that the laser and cameras are pointed in the right directions?"

Max nodded as she extricated herself from beneath the workbench. "Will do. Give me one sec." The engineer circled the table, stooping to sight the laser trajectory through the aperture and eyeball the view of the cameras. "Not sure we can get the entire aperture on one camera. Can you check the feeds?"

"Sure thing." Min moved from the window to her console, where the output of the four cameras monitoring the apparatus were on screen. One centered on the laser emitter, another on the artificial quartz that bisected the column of light--these appeared almost identical to previous runs. The third showed the clean room wall; where it used to capture a skewed angle of the ring, now the camera homed on the expansive center of Min's expensive mistake. "Hang on, let me adjust the zoom on camera three." Min stooped to her keyboard, bringing up the commands for camera control and resetting the view of that camera to its default. The display remained vacant, save the inside edge of the coil in the upper-left corner. A reference point, at least. "It's good enough, Max. Come in here, and let's run a power-up."

Minutes later, Max and Min were at their respective stations, and Min felt better. The power-up checklist was a normal, known thing. She hadn't ended the world. The large aperture cost the Institute millions of dollars: a rounding glitch in the organization's overall spending. In two months, no one would care. And hell, if they couldn't get Foresight demo-ready in two days, none of it mattered anyway. What she had perceived as an error, she now viewed as necessary progress. *An omelette on your plate means eggs have to break.* Of course, most people don't crack a million eggs at once.

"Cameras are live and recording," Min said.

"Telemetry is coming in from the new power components. Foresight looks ready to roll, I suppose. On your word, Min."

Min took a slow breath, trying to calm her wiggling nerves. "Power the laser."

11

SCHRÖDINGER'S DOG

The window darkened to the fluoride-red of the warning lights. A moment later, the dull green glow of the laser appeared on Min's display.

"Emitter is drawing a steady 300 milliwatts. Or three deciwatts, as the project scientist works in those units now."

"I'll remind the project engineer this test run is being recorded," Min replied, not returning the jab. "What's the regulator reporting?" She scooted her chair close to Max to watch over her shoulder. The instrumentation was sparse and included the active power draw and an estimated time before the singularity evaporated. With only the small laser engaged, no measures shifted on her dashboard, and the countdown clock stated "Infinity."

"Everything good, Min. Ready to power the aperture."

Min shuffled forward in her chair, teetering on the edge of the seat so she could lean closer to the monitor. "Okay, juice the aperture. Let's start at one gigawatt again."

Max clattered the keyboard, and the telemetry shifted. Within a blink of her eye, the power draw escalated. What Min thought had been a blank area of the display was a time series of the bottle's power output. The graph had jumped into existence when Max sent power into the metal ring. The graph showed a smooth one gigawatt draw on the bottle, and the evaporation clock changed to "9999 years."

Max snorted. "That a level of confidence could come from only Bruce."

"Well, I hope for the sake of this project and our jobs that it isn't just bluster. Ramp up to two gigawatts."

The engineer's fingers tattered across the keys, and the scale of the time series shifted. "Reporting two gigawatts of draw. No measurable flux." Max flipped through another page of instrumentation. "Everything looks calm."

Min turned to the camera feeds. "No change I can see in the output image. Alright, increase aperture feed to five." Her gaze shot back to Max's console in time to watch the countdown clock drop 5000 years. The power output graph adjusted to the new scale, showing the immediate and dramatic rise.

"Not even a blip," Max reported. "Steady flow of power."

Satisfied, Min returned to her station and checked the screens. "No variation in the image output. I'm unsure of the power we'll need before the ring imprints on the laser."

"Got a guess?" Max asked.

Min did some math in her brain. "Around 1800 gigawatts." An absurd amount of energy, more than conventional systems could produce over years, much less continuously provide. Almost 20 times the load that Bruce achieved field testing in his own lab. "We'll work our way there. Step up to 10."

Max confirmed, reported the evaporation timer dropping to 2999 years, but Min saw no shift in the images.

"Double it."

Again, no noticeable changes, while the evaporation clock halved in time once more. The women continued, redoubling the power consumption with each step, and finding the same results: no shift in the graph, and a shorter countdown. When they reached 1280 gigawatts, the clock dropped to 78 years, and a telemetry warning chimed from Max's terminal.

"What's wrong?" Min asked. "What's that about?"

Max bounced to the second page of instrumentation, then the third. Min's chest tightened when the engineer shot upright in her chair.

"Acoustic sensors again."

"What the hell?" Min cursed. She stood and looked through the safety glass of the clean room window. "Did something break?"

"No," Max said in a tentative voice. "No, this is different. Sustained sound." Min jumped when Max opened the comms between the two rooms and a watery gurgle of white noise sputtered through the control room monitors.

"What is that?" Min asked. "Should we shut down?"

Max clattered through her dashboards. "Nothing's showing out of bounds."

"Are the sensors faulty?"

"Not unless our ears are too," Max replied, pointing with her chin at the warbling static coming from the speaker.

Min nodded. Her brain cataloged possibilities. Power cycles from the aperture being picked up by the microphones? Could the new ring be rattling on its footing?

"Any change in power draw? Any motion on sensors?"

"All telemetry is solid, Min. No movement detected on seismic. Do you see anything on visual?"

Min's eyes blinked at her monitor. She skimmed the camera views on the Foresight device. Laser was fine, crystal was intact. The camera trained on the aperture, though, showed something strange. A yellow halo rippling away from the green beam. The flares tumbled and squirmed as if refracting through water.

"What is this?" Min had whispered before remembering she was being recorded. "Visual aberrations within the aperture noted at 1280 gigawatts."

Max's head swiveled between Min's display and her own. "What do you want to do, Min?"

Min stopped to think, torn between chasing the anomaly and preventing disaster. "How's our power source?"

"Steady, we have plenty of room to grow," Max reported.

"And all instrumentation is within expectations?"

"All except for acoustics. On the dashboards, Foresight looks fine."

Min swallowed. "Then increase the feed to 1600 gigawatts."

She didn't hear Max confirm, but Min could tell she had done it. The halo around the laser grew, widening into arcs that spiraled towards the metal ring. The beam itself remained unaffected, passing through the aperture without being obliterated.

"We're still not imprinting the laser," Min thought aloud. "And we've never been able to see what happens inside the aperture when we use it. This might be normal."

"As normal as it gets around here," Max added. "We're reading fine across the board still."

Min watched the light show for several breaths. It was a lovely display she didn't understand, and that scared her.

"Kill the laser," she said. "Maybe this light show is a side effect of imprinting photons.

Max entered the command to close the power relay to the laser. The window shading and safety lights deactivated in response. Both women gazed at the aperture on the screen. The blobs of swirling glow remained, flaring out from the center of the aperture.

"The visual halos are present without the laser," Min said aloud for the session recording.

"Christ, look at the ring, Min!"

Her gaze shifted to the window, crystal clear with the laser disabled. From this angle, their view of Foresight was oblique instead of straight-on. The aperture moved, bent the way a desert road shifts in summer. *Why aren't the safety sensors in the clean room screaming for an emergency shutdown?*

"Any other alarms, Max?"

"None," the engineer reported. "All sensors reading nominal."

Min regarded the light show with an anxious reverie.

"What's the plan?" asked Max. "We're still about 200 gigawatts shy of 1800."

Min felt it. Like sensing a ledge in the trail hike at night, or how animals feel an earthquake before it arrives. A precipice to something enormous. Potential danger or wonder or both.

"Increase power to target level," she said.

Min held her breath as the lab stilled. The hiss and warble from the speakers faded away, and the webs of light projecting on the polymer paneling lost their shape and motion.

"Reporting a steady 1800 gigawatts going into the aperture," Max stated.

Min expected more--more flash, more boom, more *something*. Instead, the resulting calm of the room knotted in her gut. "Acknowledge 1800 gigawatts, reporting cessation of auditory anomalies. Visuals-," She glanced at her monitor and gasped.

There was movement inside of the aperture. Clear and detailed, framed by the fluid edge of the ring. An organic motion Min recognized on sight.

"Max? Tell me you're seeing this too!"

Max's chair rattled as she scooted next to Min. Her heaving breath was audible. "I... I knew it!"

Min turned to her friend. "I owe you an apology, Max. I don't understand how." Her hand went to the screen, as if to pet the head of the dog framed in the aperture's opening. "But that *is* Neils Bork."

Max huffed, puffing out her lips. A new sound emitted from the speakers, the sniffling of the dog's dark snout as it probed the aperture. Then a moist click as it tasted the air with its tongue.

Max was up. Running around the desk to the clean room door. Min stretched for her, nabbing the hem of her shirt between her fingers but lacking the hold to stop her. "Max, don't! There's almost a thousand fission reactors of energy flowing through there!"

Max was not hearing it. Or she didn't care. She reached the door and slammed the handle down.

With the clean room breached, the safety protocols dropped like a guillotine: all power couplings snapped closed. Min expected to hear a *zap*, an electric jolt. But there wasn't even a whisper over the sound of the door clicking open. She checked Max's instrumentation dashboard: the bottle output was now zero gigawatts. Min scanned the camera feed of the aperture where she had seen the framed visage of the lab's former mascot.

No shimmer, no halo, no lapping tongue of Neils Bork. Just Max's hands probing the air, clutching for the ghost of her dog.

12

Size Matters

A haze smothered the morning, the sky mimicking Min's bright but diffuse thoughts and making it difficult to focus. Taking a pull from her travel mug, the last of her coffee washed over her tongue. That made two travel mugs consumed, which was twice her normal limit. The caffeine wasn't helping her mind or her mood, but she needed it to function today. As she trudged through campus, she stopped at the little overpriced coffee kiosk in the central courtyard.

Her gaze fixated on the barista's movements as he prepared her drink. Min had slept like shit. The events of the previous day iterated in her brain like a hamster waddling in a squeaking wheel, preventing proper rest. Part of her bubbled with fear—they were manipulating forces they didn't understand, and the results had been extreme. Max's dead dog appearing in the aperture? How was that possible?

And the piece of her that wasn't frightened? The all-in scientist? It blazed with excited energy. Min wanted nothing more than to repeat the experiment. Verify outcomes. Hypothesize. Test. Analyze. Repeat, until they had a better understanding of what Foresight was doing and how. And the more she listened to that inner scientist, the more she wanted to explore. And that terrified her, too. There was always risk in discovery. The trick—and the goal—was to understand. Probe. Poke whatever it was with a stick, record what happens.

Except the things they were poking included the subatomic foundations of matter and reality. And black holes. If the aperture could show Max her dead dog, what else was it capable of?

With her mug fresh with light roast, she plodded back to the research complex. From the outside, every building at Daft was identical: a one-story, glass-walled lobby containing a security gate to a bank of elevators. The bulk of the structures extended far underground.

As the elevator opened on level 31, Min could see the door to the Foresight lab was ajar. Max either arrived super-early today, or, more likely, never went home yesterday.

She confirmed her assumption upon entering the lab. Max wasn't in the control room, yet the clutter of soda cans, energy bar wrappers, and hand tools told a story of Max working through the night. But working on what?

Through the window, Min found the answer. The workbench was gone, as was the entire Foresight telescope. Instead, she found the lanky frame of a scorpion crane: a robotic carrier used to transport heavy objects around the Institute. Similar to the engine block dolly Min's father used in his hobby auto garage, except this one could lift and move around 16 metric tons of weight.

In its grip hung a monstrosity of an aperture. Several meters in diameter, the ring was two hand-widths thick. Woven through its untarnished silver gleam was at least three kilometers of vanadium dioxide cable. The colossus hung from the stinger of the crane, secured by the scorpion's vice claws. The size of it—the amount of materials that Max must have consumed during fabrication—left a tingle of awe in Min's chest.

"What the hell did you do, Max?"

The engineer appeared in the window. Max's eyes sagged, the surrounding makeup more smudge than smoke. Pinpricked pupils and cheeks drawn from the overconsumption of stimulants and a lack of rest. The odor of the coffee turned acrid then, and Min set the travel mug next to her terminal.

"What did you do?" she repeated, assuming comms were open between the rooms.

"Um... good morning?" Max's tentative voice came out of the desk speakers while her mouth moved behind the window. "Yeah, so... remember how the fabricators can auto-scale?"

Min didn't respond, but stepped closer. The aperture rested inside a polymer footing on the lab floor and rose to Max's shoulder. The engineer took a step from the window and made a *tada* motion with her hands. She tried a smile, but her eyes remained exhausted.

"What were you thinking? How much material did you consume? How did you bypass our quotas?" The questions hit fast and furious, and Max held up her palms in surrender.

"Let me explain, okay? Come into the clean room."

Min folded her arms.

"Min?"

Max's eyes were pleading. Min knew whatever she did overnight was not logical. It had nothing to do with getting Foresight ready for its demo. This was a pure expression of her angst and hope. It was a very Max thing to do.

Min entered the clean room, slamming the door. Greeting her was a stout robot. Six spindly legs secured thick-treaded tires to a narrow frame just over a meter long, on which sat an array of cameras, sensor modules, and communication devices. Min recognized it from the inter-lab show-and-tells the Institute mandated every month. Known around the Daft Institute as a "BigWheels"—an autonomous rover designed to enter and evaluate dangerous environments. It could operate from its on-board AI to map out a space on its own, identify dangers and targets, and report back to the humans safe behind its operations console. This one carried a swath of components along its blocky backbone: sensors for air quality and material sampling, plus sonar and lidar. A mechanical arm jutted from the neck of the carbon fiber beast, its end capped with directional microphones and several types of cameras.

"Oh, Max. What are you thinking?"

The engineer melted against the safety glass. "I think this is the next logical step."

"There is nothing logical about this, Max. We're supposed to be prepping the demonstration for the military."

"We'll have a demo. Just not the one Waffel is expecting."

"Max-"

"Look," she interrupted, heaving herself forward and removing something from her front pocket. "Look at what I found last night after you left." Min accepted the weightless envelope of paper. Min's skeptical gaze fell, her thumb prying open the flap to find a few strands of white fuzz. "That's fur, Min. My dog's fur. It was on the work-bench, near the ring."

She closed the envelope and handed it back. "Max, there's dog hair all over the bed by your desk-"

"I know, but this is fresh. I know it sounds odd, but I can sniff the difference, okay? This came from Neils Bork, *through* the aperture."

Min studied her friend. Exhaustion blanched her pallor and sagged on her shoulders.

"Matter passed through the aperture!" Max restated.

Min had empathy for Max's thought process. The engineer wanted to believe what she was saying. However, Min understood Foresight relayed information from one photon and imprinted it on another.

She always viewed its operation as an exchange of energy. At least, that's how Waffel had described it. "Matter from where, though?"

Max shrugged. She flapped a hand at the BigWheels. "I think we should find out."

Min's gaze followed the gesture, registering the rover pointed at the aperture opening. The footing under the ring, she realized, was a ramp.

"You want to fire it up again? Send the robot into the aperture?"

"Yes."

"But the aperture destroys whatever passes through it, Max. Like the laser."

"And yet," Max replied, tapping the envelope before wadding it in the front pocket of her cargo pants, "I'm finding my dog's hair on our clean room workbench. Plus, something cracked the indestructible polymer casing of the optics array, remember? That microscopic extra-solar bullet we can't trace to a source? I figure it must have come through the tiny aperture we were using."

Min swallowed the tingle of anticipation in her throat—the prickle that preceded powerful ideas that led to champagne breakthroughs or career-ending failures. The difference would be rigor. Identifying assumptions and testing them. And Max was making a lot of assumptions. She gazed at the aperture. The girth of it was imposing, its weight enough to pulverize bones if the scorpion crane failed. "How did you get past the material quotas to build this big-ass thing?"

Max shuffled close to Min, laying her head into the physicist's shoulder. "Remember how I said Bruce needed help with the fabricators? When he printed a bazillion keyboards?"

Min nodded, biting her nervous tongue to give Max the safety she needed to explain.

"He gave me his passkey to the fabricators so I could cancel that work order for him. He never changed it after that."

"So you-"

"I did," Max interrupted. "This beauty *technically* belongs to the Power Systems R&D lab. I ordered it on their dime, using Bruce's access."

"Oh, shit." Max had just admitted to committing several policy violations that could end their employment. Or worse, get them into legal trouble.

The engineer raised her head and stepped through the ring, turning and placing a hand on the outer coil. "I'm sure they can recycle it into... something. Besides, Waffel already laid out the consequences for not delivering." She shrugged, her other hand finding the ring as she leaned into it. "What is the Institute going to do, shit-can us twice?"

"They'll sue us into oblivion!"

Max swatted away the concern. "They'd have to acknowledge the crap material protocols, and the board will demand a failure audit. You see them taking the risk to the stock price? You think Waffel would put her own future in jeopardy? To squeeze blood from two jobless stones?"

The tentative logic relied on erratic human emotions. "I don't know, Max."

"Well, we're beyond ambivalence to an idea, because this," she slapped the ring, sending an odd clatter through the lab, "is real. It's wired up, waiting for power. And the BigWheels is ready to rumble."

Min sighed. Working from emotion was very on-brand for Max. She was stuck, and Min needed the engineer unstuck before they could pull a demo together.

"We'll be done in 30 minutes," Max pleaded. "Another half hour to reset the lab. I promise."

Min massaged her temple, muddling the words into her brain.

"Besides," Max continued, "aren't you curious about what we'll find?"

13

Champagne Moment

Minutes later, the BigWheels sat powered and awaiting commands, and electrons were flowing into the ring. The women had walked the power up to 1.8 terawatts, when the first trace of visual aberrations appeared.

"Reporting halos, like the previous session," Min said. "Anything on acoustics?"

"Yes, acoustic sensors are picking up that static again. Want to hear it?"

"Sure." Min didn't understand the visual and acoustic artifacts. There was comfort in their reproduction, though. It was a precursor to understanding them.

Once powered, the speakers spilled a wet crackle around the women. "Way louder than before," Max hollered. She lowered the volume to a comfortable level.

Min checked the cameras. Half the screen presented the feed from a stationary camera pointed into the aperture. The other half offered a view from the opposite side, with the BigWheels centered in the ring. At the moment, both revealed gold rings rippling out from the ring's center and fading near the metal edge.

"Let's step up gradually," Min said. Her best guess at their target power was 2.6 terawatts. Maybe higher. "Ramp to two terawatts."

Max confirmed two terawatts of stable power flowing through the ring. The ripples tightened inside of the aperture, reaching all the way to the edge. From the reverse view, the lines and curves of the rover bent, as if melting onto the lab floor; however, the front view confirmed the automaton was intact and solid.

"Bump it to 2.2." Before Max could acknowledge the change, Min felt it in her stomach: a sustained rumble that carried up from the floor. "Do you feel that?"

"I do," Max confirmed. She clacked through some screens, reporting, "Seismic sensors show nothing. Power is steady."

"Okay, go to 2.4," Min said.

In the next moment, the gut-rattling stilled. The speakers went silent. Min had been watching her screens, but did not see the transition: the ripples and deformations were gone. The interior of the aperture was solid and dark.

The women quieted as well, taking in the data.

Max broke the silence with a breathy exhale. "It worked."

The words pulled Min away from the strangeness on her screen. "Max, check this out." Her lab partner scooted close, leaning over her shoulder. On the forward view, the rover sat facing the aperture, the tiny LEDs on its various chassis components blinking against the shadows in the ring. The reverse view showed inky blackness. No BigWheels or LED flashes. Just the aperture filled with a dark miasma.

"Holy shit," Max whispered. After a few moments of scrutinizing the darkness, she snatched up the BigWheels control tablet and tapped. Several tight beams of white light exploded from the Big-Wheels, spilling against the aperture and the strange space beyond it.

Max scuttled next to Min, and they peered at the screens again. In the forward view, light spilled through the ring, revealing the familiar tile floor of the clean room beyond. The reverse view showed only darkness.

"That looks like our lab," Max said. "That's standard Daft Institute flooring. It's in all the labs and corridors. I've crawled under it enough to recognize it anywhere."

Min had to agree. And yet... "Does it appear fuzzy to you?"

Max nodded, her chin nudging Min's shoulder. "Dusty. Like the air purifiers are off." She held up the rover control panel--a small tablet that could send commands and receive sensor and camera feeds over the Device Operations Wireless Network. "We've got a steady data stream. I'm moving the BigWheels in."

"Wait, don't we-"

"Wait? For what?" Max's impatience dripped from her voice.

"At least check the bottle. Is it stable? Are we at risk of evaporating the singularity?"

Max huffed, palming the tablet, while her attention shot to her console. She pointed to the power instrumentation, which reported a consistent flow of 2.4 terawatts and five years until evaporation. "It's good, Min. No reason to wait."

Min wanted to double-check everything first. Verify the sensor arrays were working. But she knew scientific rigor would not still Max's emotional currents. With reluctance, Min nodded.

The smile relaxed Max's exhausted face as she rose and walked to the window. Min followed, watching over Max's shoulder as she thumbed the on-screen joystick. The BigWheels responded without pause or noise, tires easing the robot up the ramp.

The women watched the rover enter the ring. It didn't come through the other side. From their vantage, with a side view of the ring, the BigWheels had disappeared.

Min backpedaled and checked her monitor. The forward camera showed the BigWheels moving away, into the unlit lab space. If she hadn't witnessed this, she would never have believed it. "The Big-Wheels crossed through the aperture."

"I've still got a decent connection," Max reported. "Whatever's happening doesn't appear to block electromagnetic signals."

Min watched the rover's cameras on the tablet as Max tapped through the simple interface. Telemetry streams came to life, the rover reporting the baselines of various sensor components: particulate sampler, radiation detection, global positioning, and so on. With its initialization complete, the automaton scanned the environment, giving the AI input it would use to define priority targets for analysis. Its cameras were for human eyes; the BigWheels AI relied on a series of infrared and sonar sensors to evaluate its physical surroundings. Its computer induced concepts from the data and mapped them on the visual feeds, allowing the human operator to experience what the rover "saw" and help clarify or elaborate details. Shapes became objects, sounds identified as sources of movement, signs and placards translated into text. At that moment, the AI reported an empty room nine meters square, with a single door and window.

"Can you show a reverse view from the rover? What does it look like from there?"

Max panned the rover camera around, revealing a circle of light floating in space. The edge of the disk diffused into the surrounding gray.

Min wiped a hand down her face. "It's just a hole in the air."

"And it's our clean room," Max said. More data arrived: air quality samples, temperature, and other environmental measurements. "Eleven degrees Celsius. The recyclers should keep it at a steady sixteen. And it's dirty as hell. Rover's picking up dust, ozone, even some heavy metals."

"What is this?" Min asked. The question was rhetorical, yet the tablet in Max's hands replied with an alert.

"Acoustic data," Max announced. "The AI thinks it's organic. I'm giving BigWheels permission to path-find a route to the source."

On the tablet, a waypoint appeared projected onto the camera feed, the rover reporting an estimated distance-to-source of four meters. "It's just on the other side of our clean room wall," Min said. Then, correcting herself, "I mean, *that* clean room wall."

The rover's electric engine engaged, and the wheels pivoted the robot around the tear hanging in the air of this strange, filthy room. Positioned in front of the door, BigWheels raised its armature, levered the handle down, then slid forward, pushing the door open.

The rover lights spilled into the room beyond, splaying across a dual-console desk. The same terminal layout as the women shared. It left no doubt in Min's mind that this was the Foresight lab. BigWheels continued on, homing on the source of the sound.

It stopped at the fraying dog bed tucked next to Max's side of the desk. On the camera view, the AI overlaid object definition of what it thought it saw: CANIS LUPUS FAMILIARIS. A Labrador Retriever. The camera showed its head lowered, with unfocused eyes over sunken cheeks.

Max tapped the microphone on the tablet, enabling the rover speakers. "Neils?! Neils Bork?"

The dog's eyes lightened. He lifted his face and tremored.

Max's pulse heated the air next to Min.

"He looks sick," Max gasped. "Or injured."

The image of the dog froze. So did the women's breathing. Across the black glass of the control tablet, a red box appeared with penetrating white letters: Connection Lost.

Max was moving, but Min snagged her sweater, practically yanking the small woman off her boots. "You can't open the door, you'll kill the power system and close the aperture. Remember what happened last time?"

The engineer pulled loose, shaking her head as she retorted, "I disabled the safety protocols before we started."

Min froze, aghast, unable to move past the idea that Max would risk their lives and keep it to herself.

Max's words came through the speakers as the door shut behind her: "I'm going to get my dog!"

14

TESTING BOUNDARIES

"Bork? Bork?! Come to me, sweetie." Max stooped, trying to project her voice around the active aperture thrumming with electricity. She retreated from the ring and checked the rover's control tablet. It still showed the same frozen image of her dog. The same error message of a lost connection to the BigWheels. And the tablet remained unresponsive. "Damn this thing!"

"Take a breath, Max." Min was beside her now, a hand on her shoulder. "Let's think through our next steps. Does the rover have a failsafe protocol? Like, will it return to where it started if it loses communications?"

"I... I don't know," Max replied. "It's just a fancy remote controlled toy with sensors on it to me."

Min shrugged and did that thing with the corner of her mouth: a surrender to the unknowable. "I guess we should check the documentation."

Max felt her face tighten. Min was being Min. Careful. Thoughtful. Logical. Good things, but useless standing in front of a magical door to an unexplainable chance to reunite with her most beloved friend. There was no logic here. This was an opportunity for the impossible. A gift Max had no intention of leaving unopened.

"Min, I appreciate you. And you're going to hate what I'm about to do."

Before the disappointment could sour her friend's face, Max bolted through the ring. She expected a tingle, some nausea or disorientation. There was nothing of the sort. One step through a ring of metal humming with more power than humans had ever consumed, and Max found herself in eerie quiet.

She almost peed when something slammed against her back.

"Sorry," Min said, stumbling upright and using Max for support. "Sorry, I kind of clenched my eyes and followed you."

Max had shut her eyes, too. A blink as she leaped through the ring, more reflex than the fear bubbling in her head. Her tired eyes were open now, taking in a layout identical to the room they had left: the safety glass looking into the control room, and the door next to it. Airborne dust was palpable, leaving a tang on her tongue. "It tastes like dirty air filters," she noted.

"You've licked a dirty filter?"

"No, dumbass. But you get how space takes on a flavor? Around food and stuff?"

"I know," Min conceded, "I know, sorry. I'm nervous. Making jokes."

Max smiled, reached out, and took Min's hand in hers. "I'm about to do nervous things, too," she said. "I might vomit."

She turned to the aperture, spinning Min around with her. It appeared as in the video feed from the BigWheels—a glowing circular viewport on their clean room, hovering over the floor. The perspective of this ruined lab aligned with their own, and Max spent a moment taking in the odd shift in view.

"It's a magic mirror, in a way." She leaned, watching more of the clean white lines and tile flooring of that room replace the dank greys of this room. "Mirror, mirror in the air, show me my lab in disrepair."

Min's hand tightened, then released. "Except the magic mirror doesn't let you walk through it. Can we get Bork and the rover, and head home?"

Max swallowed, her mouth sticky from sudden nerves, and she moved to the window. The rover blocked her the view of the dog bed. She eased through the control room door, calling to her dog. As Max scuttled between the BigWheels and the wall, she passed the tablet to Min. "Here, see if you can get this piece of crap working."

Her short legs vaulted over the front fenders of the BigWheels, and Max caught her first glimpse of him. He was curled tight in his bed, in a position she called "the dumpling" where all four feet tucked against his chest, and his tail rested across his side, giving him the shape of the gyoza Max often enjoyed in the cafeteria.

Could this be him?

The dog's head wobbled, his ears and eyebrows shifting with unfocused curiosity. His snout rose as he turned to Max.

The dog was shell-shocked, a thousand-meter stare piercing her but not seeing her. His cheeks sunk against his teeth, and sharp ridges of bones protruded everywhere. Brow, vertebrae, ribs, even his paws were emaciated.

"Neils Bork," she cooed. "It's me, honey. It's Maxine." She stooped on her haunches.

The Labrador remained unfocused, yet his ears piqued. His nose wiggled at her, tracing a wobbly line between them. His front legs unfolded, and the dog heaved to a sitting position. They were eye-to-eye.

"The rover seems fine," Min blurted behind her. "Control software is responsive again, the connection re-established. Not sure what happened."

Max spoke over her shoulder, "Just hang tight a minute, Min." Neils Bork stood up on all fours, shaking with stress. Gazing at her with a new glint in his eyes. Recognition. And the disbelief that Max felt in herself.

She raised a hand, splayed her fingers. Neils Bork eased his muzzle beneath them, as if testing if Max was a mirage or figment of his mind. When her skin touched his fur, the dog lurched forward. His weight leaned into her. Lighter than she remembered, yet familiar. Head into her arm, his side careening into her chest until Max had to sit on the floor to keep from falling over.

And then the most pitiful noise came from the dog: a whine of desperation and grief, amplified by the still and filthy air. With eyes brimming, Max buried her face into his shoulder, inhaling the dusty sweet odor she knew as home.

"Oh my God," she wept. "I can't believe you're real."

15

Tomorrow's Problems, Today

Ten minutes passed while they poured out their feelings, and Min waited as the dog and Max took each other in. Max cried while Neils Bork tasted his human's face. His tail engaged, wagging with a ferocity that crescendoed into his signature Bork-butt wiggles. While this played out, Min ran diagnostics on the BigWheels, finding nothing amiss. She checked the tablet, which reported normal operational status as well. So Min dug deeper.

She found something impossible.

With Max calm and rubbing the belly of the dog cantilevered on her lap, Min revealed her findings.

"The BigWheels and tablet are fine. Diagnostics are all clean. Since wherever we are seems to be the Daft Institute, I wondered if the rover could detect any of the internal wireless networks."

Max's ruddy eyes rose with curiosity. "Did it locate any?"

Min nodded, checking the list of networks on the tablet. "I thought this place might have something similar to our DOWN." The Device Operations Wireless Network was a communication system available throughout the campus. Robots used it to coordinate their atomic clocks, GPS positioning, and near-term logging and instrumentation. Its major benefit was that the receivers could pull their power from the wireless signal itself. "As it turns out, there is a DOWN compatible with our rover."

"No way!" Max's smile carried into her eyes. A face Min hadn't seen in months. "Can it connect?"

"Yes, and it did. Connected without fuss, in fact. And that's where things get weird."

"Weirder, you mean."

Min swallowed. She bit her lip. "Everything has been pretty normal compared to what I'm about to tell you."

The smile broadened, rounding her cheeks. Max loved puzzles, which was good, because Min had found a doozy.

"GPS reports our position as the Daft Institute. Our physical location doesn't seem to have changed going through the aperture."

Max nodded, saying, "That checks out. What else?"

Unsure how to say it, Min took a moment to tap through the tablet interface. When the device's atomic clock was on the screen, she turned it to Max. "According to the Institute's official clock, we're almost one year in the future."

"What?" Max laughed.

Min pointed at the date on-screen.

"What?" Max repeated with a shade of worry as her smile withered.

"But that makes no sense, does it? How are we in the *future* if Neils Bork is alive, Max?"

Max blinked, shook her head as if clearing a mental fog. "Wait. You're a few steps ahead of me. You're saying Foresight sent us into the future? It's a time machine?"

Min felt her cheeks flush. "I don't know. That's not how I understand the aperture, but..."

"What is it?" Max prodded.

"Temporal physics isn't my bag. Not at all. I can't comprehend what's happened. We've used the Foresight technology in a novel capacity. No one's ever dumped 2.2 terawatts into a two meter aperture.

And quantum physics is... well, it's creepy. I prefer to stick to the simpler parts of it."

"Simple stuff? Such as photon entanglement?"

"Exactly," Min replied. She realized the engineer's sardonic wit when Max's eyebrow rose into that expression Min called her "Spock face." "Look, I'm just reporting what I'm seeing here, Max. This place is a year from... well, today."

Her friend's tight curls bobbed in rhythm to the belly scratches she was giving Bork. "Okay," Max said. "Anything else?"

Now Min got the chance at sarcasm. "Is that not enough for you?"

"I mean, sure, it's strange. No question. I just don't understand why you're telling me this. A few minutes ago, you wanted to grab Bork and the BigWheels and go home." Max gazed into the shimmering blue-white glow spilling through the window, the light from the past illuminating this wrecked future. "Now you're in data-collection mode. I know you—you don't make that kind of mental shift unless you have a theory."

Min licked her lips, tasting the tang of metal and dust and realizing that Max had been right: this room had a taste. "Does this place seem operational to you? Does it strike you as active, or abandoned?"

Max chuckled and looked around. Remnants of their day-to-day work lay strewn across the floor, and a layer of grime stuck to everything. "I'd say it's deserted, except for Neils Bork, here." She leaned over, sucking in another sniff of the dog's raised foot with a serene hum.

"Yeah. So, between today and a year from today, our lab turns into this." She gestured to the surrounding filth. "This doesn't look good."

"You want to know what happened? Or I mean, what happens? Between now and then?"

Min gulped down the lump of nerves in her throat. "Yeah, I do. I'm pulling whatever logs I can discover on the DOWN. There aren't a lot. I'd like to snoop around, see what we can learn."

Max shifted her boots under her, then heaved Bork the rest of the way off her lap before standing. "We could send the rover exploring," she offered. "Cover more ground, collect more data."

Min smiled, returning the tablet to Max. "Already configured for autonomous exploration. Prioritized to find people and names. Can you double check my settings?"

Max's stare bounced over the screen, and her finger followed as she verified things. "Looks good. This will map out the space. Search for anyone here. Notify us of any biological, chemical, or radiological dangers. It may turn up some answers."

Min agreed and gestured at their workstations. "I also want to power our machines here. Pull our files and whatnot for the last year. Take them back with us to review later."

Max's eyes widened. "That's smart." Her gaze scanned to the darkness in the open door leading out of the Foresight lab. "The building's primary systems appear offline. If we had a portable power source, I could connect the control room to it."

"What about the rover?"

Max shook her head. "It uses a hardened battery on a closed circuit. If I had attached a power share module, we could tap its battery. As configured, this BigWheels battery isn't accessible."

Min sighed.

"I mean, this is the Daft Institute, right? So, no prizes for guessing where we'll find a power source."

Min nodded. "I was hoping you'd say something along those lines. Why don't I head to Power Systems and hunt for a battery or generator?"

"Or a power bottle," Max suggested. "Like Bruce said, 'Why mess with one black hole when you can mess with two?' If we're sticking around, I want to feed this poor dog. He's got to be thirsty, too."

Min grimaced as she gave the lab a cursory visual search. "I see nothing here. Not sure I'd eat the left-behinds, anyway. Check the cafeteria for something canned."

Minutes later, the BigWheels was exploring the distressed hallways of the building. While Min monitored the automaton, Max located a half-charged tablet among the ruined lab. With the powered networks unavailable, she rigged up a chat interface using the limited capabilities of the DOWN. Not ideal, but voice comms required computers that weren't powered at the moment. This would enable rudimentary communication once they separated.

The three left the lab together, skulking down the corridor towards the junction to the cafeteria. After squeezing Min's hand, Max turned down an adjoining hallway, with Bork following. Min continued straight towards the stairwell.

As Min reached for the door to the stairs, her tablet chimed. She expected a "be careful" message from Max, so it surprised her to find a note from BigWheels. Across the top third of the screen, a calming blue banner carried reassuring white letters that filled Min with a bloom of hope and a tickle of dread.

Priority text identified: WAFFEL. See attachment for source image. See map for waypoint WAFFEL-01.

The rover had located the word "Waffel" in one of its cameras as it moved through the corridors. Min tapped the link in the notification, and the tablet display filled with the photo from the rover. It was a black glass placard, the kind used to identify labs and offices in the endless intersecting hallways. Min mouthed the words as she read them in her head.

E. SHAUNA WAFFEL - CHIEF SCIENTIST, APPLIED QUANTUM
LOGISTICS.

Chief Scientist? Her title had been Senior Director of some-
thing-or-other. A management career track, whereas Chief Scientist
was a technical role for individual contributors and actual scientists
like Min. She wondered what Machiavellian tactics the woman used
to get herself transitioned into that title so fast. There was no way she
was qualified.

Career politics aside, Min knew her advisor would have information. She expanded the rover's map, finding Waffel's office pinned with
a green dart. It was in the opposite direction. Past the Foresight lab,
then down a corridor to the right.

Min let the door close behind her and typed a quick message to
Max: *Change of plans. Big Wheels found Waffel's office. Heading there
first.* She included brief directions from their lab, since Max didn't
have access to the rover telemetry on her device.

Min waited for a response from Max before moving. It came in a
few seconds: *Be careful. Safe bet Future Waffel is an a-hole, too.*

16

TRIBES

Her cleated boots clunked against the floor. They should have squeaked—on clean tiles, they made the sound of a thumb scraping across an over-inflated balloon. Max stopped at the next junction and toed the grime, eyeballing the greasy dust padding her steps. Bork paused at her side, heeling like a good boy.

She lifted her gaze and studied the choice of hallways. The Institute labeled doors, but that was about it. So, if you needed to get somewhere, you had to know where it was. Augmented digital maps were available over the wireless network. Unfortunately, with no current network available, Max was relying on the layout of this building being identical to the one she knew, where parallel and intersecting hallways of the Research Complex mapped out like city blocks. If one corridor was inaccessible, they could try another. .

According to her internal compass, the cafeteria should have been a straight jog ahead. However, Max found the way blocked by desks, chairs, and equipment piled up for no discernible reason other than to impede movement through the halls. Rather than climb through it, she would reroute their way around. The strategy would keep them heading towards their goal, but on a circuitous path.

At the next junction was another barricade, this one composed of spot-welded sheet metal and impassible without tools. "What the hell?" She mumbled to herself. She peered at Neils Bork as if he might have information she didn't. "I think someone's trying to keep folks out of the cafeteria."

Which made sense in a few scenarios. The cafeteria had organic fabricators—devices that could assemble edible meals out of the core nutritional materials stored there. The barricades would protect those resources. Or hoard them. If that was the case, it meant something bad had happened here. Like, blow-humans-back-to-tribal-behavior awful.

A movie played in her mind: engineers raising their banner of a system diagram; managers carrying flags of project status colors for their corporate objectives; an epic battle of the can-dos versus the how-you-should-have-done-its. As a concept, it was comical, but seeing evidence of it chilled her from the inside.

"Let's keep going, boy," she said as she gave Bork a solid head-scratching. "Maybe we can squeeze through one of the sloppier barriers." The dog's eyes were serious, tracking Max like it was their job. As she retreated the way they came, he fell in step beside her. Max relished having Bork pacing her, but it took conscious effort to slow her stride so the weakened dog could keep up.

At the next hallway intersection, Max evaluated the dome of polymer molded chairs stacked three meters high. She gave one a mild tug and the entire pile shifted in response. If they tried to move the precarious stack, or burrow through it, they'd get stuck or injured. They traipsed on, finding the corridor to their right open, and followed it to another makeshift rampart.

A mountain of long picnic benches with connected seats, solid things made of fancy materials that repelled germs, stains, and odors. Whoever had constructed this obstacle had interleaved the chairs, locking them together and limiting their movement. Max analyzed the perimeter of the blockage, searching for gaps near the walls. She found a slot Bork might squeeze through, but nothing large enough for her.

And Max was small. It came in handy around the Institute, for the same reasons children worked during the Industrial Revolution: someone needed to fit inside the tight metal guts of the machines to fix them when they broke. Maybe not the ringing endorsement for slight statures Max wanted, but thin fingers, wiry arms, and a narrow torso meant Max could fit into spaces others could not.

The thought became an idea.

Every floor in the Institute covered a hollow used to carry cables for power or communications. The term "crawlspace" was a misnomer, yet that's what folks around the Institute called it. Most of the staff wouldn't try to cram themselves into that tiny channel under their feet. However, Max did it all the time. Not always to run wire; sometimes it was the most straightforward way to access a secure area when she wasn't authorized.

She tapped the floor with her boot, watching for the telltale shift of a loose tile. When one near the left wall clicked, she knelt down and brushed away the dust. Her fingertips ran over the tile's flush edge, finding no grip. Normally, lifting the tiles required a special tool called a scepter (and permission from Building Operations), but everyone knew the magnetic tile locks were fickle. Many tiles would come loose with a little negative air pressure. In the lab, Max used a sink plunger she kept in the control room cabinet. This time, she licked her palm, slapped it against the smooth tile, and dragged against the suction.

The edge lifted enough for her fingernails to gain leverage before the seal on her palm broke. The tile popped out, revealing the crawlspace.

Max poked her head into the hole and checked the channel. It was clear of cables and looked clean. She rose to Bork's purposeful stare—the piercing gaze of a dog that wants to assist, even when the situation doesn't call for a dog.

"Okay, Borkster. I'm going spelunking. Then I'll help you through the fence."

His brow crested, gaze fluttering with worry as he whined. *Please don't leave me.*

"I'm not leaving you, Bork. Never leaving you. Okay?" She shifted off her knees and dropped her feet into the crawlspace. "Two minutes, and I'll be talking to you the whole time."

17

Spelunkery

Max contorted her body, feeding her legs into the dark gap, then her pelvis. Once that was done, the rest of her slipped through. All the while, she reassured the dog with calm words. On her back inside the tiny channel, she wormed forward, arms reaching up to grope her path, her torso waddling through the tight space. One tile slogged by millimeters from her nose, then another. Testing the third, she felt resistance: she had not cleared the barricade. She shimmied ahead in the claustrophobic darkness, Bork's cries growing anxious.

The next tile gave to gentle pressure. She shoved it off, relishing the breeze of air whipping into the stifling crawlspace. Her fingers gripped the lip of the opening, and she heaved herself forward. Once she wriggled free, she crossed to the far wall, to the Bork-sized gap through the barrier. Her dog was already nosing through the blockage to reach her.

His snout met her hand, and Max massaged the dog's head. She turned away from the barricade, shining her light across the dark hall and into a widening space several paces ahead.

"Let's feed you," she said. Bork licked his chops and fell in heel with her as she continued on. They entered the cafeteria proper, and it was barren. The rows of bench tables were missing, along with the smaller tabletops and their chairs—ballast for the hallway barricades, she assumed. She shone her light across the place, shadows of the empty food packaging scattered on the floor flowing in the white beam. The vacant gloom was unnerving. An expansive area to watch for dangers, especially when the tablet's LED didn't reach the far corners of the room.

Max crept towards the kitchen door with Bork as her shadow. The handle clicked open, the sound of the retracting latch reverberating in the immense emptiness. She stilled, fingers around the handle, listening to the fading echo. Straining to hear the shuffle of something moving in the dark. But she heard nothing.

She pushed the door and spun into the galley in one swift motion. Bork padded behind, sniffing the air but giving no warning of danger as he leaned into her leg. Her light splashed across stainless steel fixtures and appliances, a center island of prep stations, cooktops, and a few smaller bench-top portion fabricators.

Across the room, the door to long-term food storage hung on its hinges, an open invitation to explore. Max jogged past the machinery and sinks and into the room of floor-to-ceiling shelving.

On a routine day, canned food lined the shelves, but Max found them bare. Bork followed her, sniffing the lower racks, giving them the occasional taste with his tongue. She was ready to give up when she saw Neils Bork stick his nose under the bottom shelf, then paw at the gap. He stood up, eyes locking on hers in the universal dog face of, *Help me, human.*

She stooped, shone the light to see one flat can wedged between the shelf and the floor.

"Good boy!" she sang. The tin took effort to free, but once it was in her hand, Max flushed with elation. It was tuna: Bork's favorite! And he seemed to recognize it, his attention a targeting laser on the tin.

Max returned to the kitchen, locating a prep station that was cleaner than the others. There, she spotted a manual can opener and a bamboo plate. The items were recently used, missing the dust coating the rest of the kitchen. They were evidence that someone had holed up here.

As the opener bit into the lid, the next logical thought snapped in-place: *So where are they now?*

She stopped once more to listen for close movement or breathing. All she could hear was Bork's huffing. With airborne tuna particles, he would not calm until he had eaten. She ratcheted open the can, splatted the meat onto the plate, and set the plate on the ground.

Bork dug in, rapacious. He was usually a forager, pecking at food when he was hungry. Now he slurped the vittles as if inhaling air. It broke Max's heart, and she wondered how long he had been suffering.

Max moved to hydrate him. She twisted the sink faucet; the satisfying hiss of running water arrived as a blessing. Her gaze shot staccato over the kitchen, looking for a bowl.

At the spatter of the water in the metal sink, Bork nosed her hand. He was thirsty, and telling her so. She considered using the tuna tin as a water bowl for a moment, but the toothy edge of the can might cut his tongue.

"Screw it. Not like I can trash the place more."

Max swiped up Bork's plate from the floor, then used it to deflect water over the sink's lip. Bork bit at the falling shower for a minute before stumbling away and belching.

Over the emotional high of being reunited with her dead friend, her curiosity piqued. She checked him over, smoothing the wetness out of his fur as she scoured him from head to torso. Her fingers massaged the damp pelt on his chest, finding the wad of hard tissue she expected there. A harmless fatty growth dogs get in random spots. And evidence that this dog was 100% Neils Bork.

Her mind knotted. How was Bork alive in the future, when he died in the past? Beyond that, how had he survived with no humans around to care for him?

He licked her face with his fishy tongue when she got close enough to let him. That sensation—the sticky sandpaper of the dog's lapper on her cheeks—she wasn't aware she had missed it.

Curiosity could wait. Right now, gratitude was enough.

"Come on, boy. Let's get home," she said. She stood, and Bork padded next to her as they sneaked into the cavernous cafeteria. A few steps in, she accelerated. Ahead, staying just beyond her meager beacon of light, Max imagined the ghosts of this place running away from her. She sped up, chasing the mental specters until she reached the corridors. Then she stopped.

There were six hallways leading out from the cafeteria, and she wasn't sure which one they had used. She glanced to Neils Bork, who met her stare with a head-tilt of expectation: *You choose, Max.*

Max shrugged. The hallways interconnected. "Guess it doesn't matter," she told the dog. They moved to the closest corridor, and after a few meters, Max realized Bork was missing from her side.

She panicked until she heard his whine. She turned, the light showing her dog trembling at the hallway opening, ears pressed against his skull and eyes darting from Max to the darkness behind her.

"What is it?" she asked. Rhetorical, as the dog could not answer, and yet Bork emitted a rising cry. His version of, *Please, no.*

The sight of her anxious dog raised her hackles, the tingle running up her spine. She spun, expecting eyes on her, but the light spat into the black void of the hallway. There was nothing but dust. Walls. The floor.

She stepped deeper into the dark, listening. Hearing only her threshing pulse. After another tentative step, a shape took form just past the reach of her light.

Someone was there. A shadow sitting on the floor, its back against the wall.

"Hello?" Max said. She regretted the fear in her voice, but she could not contain it. "Hello, who's there?"

The person lay quiet and heavy as a rock. They sat still as Max's breath.

Another tread forward. Her light uncovered more of the reclined figure.

And Max screamed.

18

CONSTANT CHANGE

The place was abandoned; from the looks of the facility, Min hypothesized an evacuation. The hallways lay cluttered with trash and equipment, the largest of which the rover had pushed out of the way by brute force, or climbed over using its articulated axles. Dregs of broken equipment and furniture blocked many laboratory doors, and the accessible spaces were in the same shape as her own lab. The building appeared devoid of people.

Waffel's office wasn't where it should be. At least in Min's mental map. Her boss was management, and management worked on the upper floors, just under ground-level, close enough to the executives to receive their daily floggings and submit TPS reports. Now her space was here, meters from the Foresight lab, amid actual work getting done.

The door was closed. Min knocked and waited out of polite habit, but expected no response. After a pregnant pause, her fingers rotated the cool metal lever. The latch retracted with a scrape, and the door eased open.

The back wall was wrong. From edge to edge and ceiling to floor, there was clear glass. What Min saw in it was impossible.

A landscape. Other buildings as dreary and powerless as the one she was in. It took Min a moment to reorient. This was the Daft campus, except no longer underground. Had the Institute somehow inverted the campus? Rebuilt them over the earth instead of within it? Why would they do that? And how could they have gotten it done in so short a time? Even with modern fabrication technology, a building would take months to complete.

And more details pierced the fog in her head. It was dusky out there. Cold purples saturated the sky with warmer glows of orange and yellow shifting through it. A coherent sunset would cool away from the horizon. Here, the brightness formed waves through the darkness above, phosphorescent worms corkscrewing through a bruise.

The vision was lovely—a view of something natural and organic. And it was terrifying—so unlike anything she had ever seen. Min felt vulnerable under that sky, a speck in an immense and apathetic universe.

She forced her gaze off the scene outside and found a second horror.

Waffel was there. Seated behind her desk, facing Min. Not looking at her. Focused on nothing. Because Waffel was dead.

Min's hands went to cover her mouth. The corpse was dessicated. She wore her standard lab coat over a blouse, and pearl jewelry adorned the leathery skin of her ears and face. The Daft identity card on the lanyard around her neck dispelled any doubt. This was Shauna Waffel.

Min forced a breath, and it carried the taste of the sweat from her palms clamped over her mouth. She let her gaze fall on its own, follow the deflated billows in the lab coat down the body and to the desk. The blotter was spotless except for a small plastic capsule. It was open, the black cap set to the side, and whatever it contained was missing.

Min spied vivid red printing on the vial. A red triangle icon marked the container, the corners blunted to create an odd-looking hexagon: the Institute's universal symbol identifying mortal danger. She leaned in to read the words: LAST RESORT. Her mind boiled with speculation about what that meant, and the possibilities were gruesome. Her eyes peeled to the window. Min heaved in a breath, and her chest tightened as if the air evaporated from the room.

She struggled to focus on something outside. Anything tangible and close and real that would stave off her anxiety. She avoided the deep, strange sky. She gazed down instead at the inverted campus. At the courtyard at the center of campus. Where the barista kiosk should have stood. Except there was no ground, not that she recognized. Just long, thick strands of something spindly and woven. The pattern stuck her as organic, like the streaks in the sky above, twisting and curling around the buildings and knitting between one another. They covered every inch of visible earth.

Her panic spiked, and Min stumbled backward until she hit the wall across from Waffel's door. She needed Max to know what she'd found; Min raised the tablet.

She found four alerts waiting for acknowledgment. Three were from BigWheels, and one from Max. Her shaking fingers tapped the message from Max first.

Body in the cafeteria. Something bad happened here. Please be careful. We're hauling ass back to the lab.

Flipping through the remaining notifications revealed grisly discoveries: objects the rover considered people, or signs of people. Two bodies in the Modern Materials workshop, with images of the same mummified skin as Waffel. And a bloody handprint in one of the interleaving corridors.

Min steadied her index finger enough to peck out a reply to Max. *Waffel is dead too. Meet me outside her office. I need you to see this.*

19

Bigger is Better

The women stood in the room next to Waffel's. It shared the same window-as-a-wall feature without the mummified corpse aesthetic. Satiated with food, Neils Bork nestled into the corner closest to Max, grunting snores almost as soon as he dumplinged up.

"The entire planet looks abandoned," Max whispered. "Like everyone up and evacuated."

Min nodded, tapping the window. "See that stuff on the ground?"

Max pressed her face against the glass. Her hands cupped her eyes to block what ambient light there was. "It looks like..."

"Like what? Just say it."

"Like some kind of plant? Overgrowth, now that nobody is pruning the hedges?" She peeled away from the window, checking Min's reaction to the absurd statement. Rather than a smirk, Min shrugged with curiosity.

"I can't argue with that." Min put a finger on the window, pointing at one building just visible in the dusky light. "Now check out that structure over there. Which should be Administration and Security."

Max put her face back into her cupped hands on the glass. The building's base hid in the shadow of a massive knot of those creepy branches. From that bulb protruded spindly fingers piercing the building's facade. "Holy Moly. It's been speared."

"Assuming they made those windows of safety glass," Min said as her finger squeaked on the window, "they should withstand the direct impact of an artillery shell, Max."

She knew where Min's logic was heading. The stuff covering the ground wasn't slow overgrowth. It hadn't consumed the place once the people were gone. This was the aftermath of a single catastrophic event. The cause for humans leaving, not the result of it.

The tablet chimed, and she cursed. "I'm sick of notifications about bodies from BigWheels. This is the fourteenth one so far."

"Recall it," Max blurted, the idea still congealing in her swampy mind. "Call the rover, and let's clear a space for it at the window. The specialty cameras will reveal more detail in the low light."

"Smart," Min said, tapping a few times on the black glass before tucking the tablet into the rear pocket of her jeans. "Rover's en route. ETA is ten minutes. Let's make some room for it."

The women moved the desk to the far corner and shoved the two chairs down the hallway a few meters. The soft purr of the electric motors preceded the tablet announcing BigWheels's arrival. Max took the tablet and set a new waypoint inside of the office. BigWheel's six tires reconfigured themselves into a line, narrowing the automaton's profile enough to pass through the doorway with room to spare. Once inside, the wheels spread out into their natural positions.

As the automaton settled in the office, Neils Bork scuttled out with nervous energy and leaned into Max's leg.

It took some manual control for Max to align the optical sensors against the window. They sat at the end of an articulating arm with a single joint, making alignment difficult. "At least there's no light noise," Min stated.

"Yeah," Max replied, "this should be able to reveal a lot of detail." The sensor pod was as close to the window as the armature allowed. "Okay, BigWheels, show us what we can't see," she whispered.

Min crowded next to her, and Max opened the first sensor feed: basic optics. The display was empty, as they expected. Min cycled to the next sensor array: low-light amplification. The screen washed in a lime green that darkened with detail as the women held their breath. Their view crept deeper, more crumbling buildings crawling out of the piercing glow, the area between them filled with that sordid weave. The image blurred as the AI adapted to varying light levels.

The winding branches covered everything on the ground. Max imagined an enormous mutant space squid, with millions and millions of tentacles, trying to grab hold of and consume the planet, squeezing it into pieces small enough to fit inside its gigantic beak. A reflexive shudder ran through her, chilling her skin to gooseflesh.

"Look at that," Min pointed at the screen. Past the horizon of their view, suspended in the lime murk of the tablet display, something hovered in the air. A wide column that expanded down into the nondescript areas the rover's optics refused to process. "Can you focus on that? Wring out more detail?"

Max centered on the strange vertical shape. The sonar and rangefinders on the BigWheels were useless thanks to the window, but based on the magnification it took to frame the floating structure, Max was able to estimate how far away it was. "Whatever that is, it's in orbit."

The women sat in apneic quiet as the AI worked to clean up the image and reveal more out of the paltry light. The shades varied from vibrant Kelley to apple to lime to emerald and every other shade of green Max could name. Details pulsed in and out as the computer maximized contrast.

Min broke the silence. "Does that look like..." The colors and shadows stabilized, and the image came into a wobbly focus.

The column climbing through the haze was clearer now. Texture and depth emerged, revealing it wasn't solid, but a massive coil of fibers rising into the atmosphere, ending at a rounded cap floating above the planet.

"The tendrils all over the ground, they reach up to that enormous thing," Max confirmed. She zoomed in on the cap, the terminus of whatever these things were.

"Wait a sec," Min said. She snatched the tablet, squinting at the fuzzy oblique shape on the screen. "Oh God, no," she whispered through a closed throat as she lowered the tablet.

Max took it back, glowering over the display. "What? What is it?" But Max caught it before Min answered.

The pale greens showed a curved shape capping the tangled fibers. Bright and precise streaks of lime crossed its surface. "It's an aperture," Max croaked. "A huge Foresight aperture, in orbit. That must be kilometers across!"

Processing the situation outside, Max's head reeled. "Why would they build an aperture so big? Why did these strange tendrils push it into orbit?"

"No, no," Min said. Max turned to find her eyes hard, and then Min framed her dread into a hypothesis. "Whatever is all over the ground? I think it came *from* that aperture in the sky."

20

HONEYPOT

The three stayed close as they returned to their previous plan: ransack Power Systems and locate a portable power source; bring up the Foresight lab computers; slurp the data onto their tablets; and haul ass to their own time and figure out how to avoid this hell-scape.

They passed the Foresight lab, continued down the hall, and opened the door to the stairwell. The tiny cones of light from their tablets revealed a handful of steps leading up and down from the current landing.

"So, they extruded the buildings, right?" Max asked. Her voice rattled against the tight cement walls. "What was down should be up?"

"I don't know," Min admitted.

Max's gaze went up, and her foot tapped the step leading to the higher floors. The dog moved beside her. As they rounded the next corner on the stairs, Min took a moment to look down the slim gap created at the center of the spiraling staircase. The light showed only their wakes cutting through the floating dust.

Max waited until Min was on the landing before trying the door. The handle dropped without resistance, and the door inched open into the unknown.

Oblivious to caution, Bork nosed the gap and trotted into the hallway with a sharp tippy-tap of his dog nails. Max and Min followed.

Max tiptoed down the hall and focused her tablet light onto the glass placard of the first door they encountered.

"Power systems. Capacitor farm," she read. "We're heading the right way. R&D should be one floor up."

They returned to the stairwell and hoofed up another floor. This hallway appeared like the ones below in layout, differing only in the scattered flotsam. Max continued to lead the way with Bork, while Min followed and kept her head on a swivel.

"Here," Max said, pointing to the black glass: POWER SYSTEMS - RESEARCH AND DEVELOPMENT. "Let's see if Bruce left us any presents."

As Max wrapped her fingers on the door's handle, Min lay a cautious hand on her shoulder. "Careful. Go slow, okay?"

Max nodded, easing her weight into the door.

Min's eyes adjusted. The few meters of splashing light showed the tepid cream cubicles she expected. Max hoisted herself onto an office chair to peer over the partitions, scanning the into the gloom.

"Kill your light for a second," she said.

Min pressed the LED on the tablet against her leg to block it. "What is it?"

"A light source," she said, pointing. Min lined up her sight on the extended finger and stared into the black. Sure enough, across the void, a sickly glow reflected off of the metal cubicle frame. "Looks like a powered terminal. We're in the right place."

Max hopped off the chair. "Let's find where that power is coming from."

Navigating the maze of half-walls with only a meter of visibility was cumbersome. After a few minutes of prairie-dogging and backtracking, the women stood before the only piece of working technology they'd seen on this side of the aperture.

A monitor. Max put a finger on the screen, pointing to the customized command prompt: GOSE~>. "This is Bruce's terminal," she remarked. "It's powered, and he's still logged in."

"I wonder how long it's been sitting here, waiting for input," Min said.

Max pulled the keyboard towards her and typed. The screen filled with a log of commands with their dates and times of execution. "Last command ran about four months ago," she said. "Or nine months in the future, from our frame of reference. And look at this." Max drew a line under the last entry with her pinky: SECURE-LAB. "The last thing Bruce did was lock down his lab."

"Okay," Min said, "that makes sense. Can we trace where this terminal is getting its power?"

Max stooped under the desk, her hands following cables to a power receptacle. "This cube has a dedicated power source. I'll have to dig into the floor to trace it."

Over the next half hour, the two women pulled up partitions and floor tiles, so Max could follow the cabling to the source of the juice. Meanwhile, Bork analyzed their surroundings, staying near the humans while indulging his curious nose. The cable's path was circuitous, backtracking and crossing itself several times before it ran beneath a sealed door only ten meters from the glowing monitor.

Max huffed and stood, dusting herself off and tapping the door. "This was Bruce's personal workspace. It's where he told me about the bottle technology. Whatever is powering the terminal is behind this door. There's a power bottle in there. I'd bet money I don't have on it."

Min tried the handle, but it wouldn't give. "Guess that's what 'secure-lab' means," she mumbled. "I can search for the command that unlocks this door," she suggested, gesturing toward Bruce's terminal.

Max shrugged. "Yeah, seems like our best option. I'll poke around for another way in."

"The floor looks full," Min said. She knew Max could squeeze through the gaps in the raised flooring. Not possible here, given the cabling crammed into the space. Min hated watching Max squirm into that tight gap, and the thought of the woman's compact frame contorting through the channel designed for wires was enough to give Min claustrophobic shivers. "Please stay out of the floor. Seriously."

Max's gaze swiveled along the base of the wall they needed to bypass. "No promises."

Back at Bruce's terminal, Min examined the command history again. Most labs customized their operations with scripts. The commands were unknown to her, but their names carried their intent. She recognized the pattern—every command comprised an action and a target. For instance, Bruce scripted "secure-lab" to lockdown his lab space. Other commands from his history included "purge-cache," "test-alert," and "archive-log." It was a best practice at the Daft Institute, since it made the commands easy to remember and, to Min's benefit, discover and learn.

It also meant Min might guess how to unlock the lab. The target was "lab," she knew this from Bruce's command history. She just needed the correct action. She typed the first thing that came to mind: UNSECURE-LAB.

The terminal responded with: ERROR: UNKNOWN COMMAND. FOR A LIST OF COMMANDS TYPE GET-COMMAND.

She entered the suggestion, reeling at the ream of data returned. The sucking snap of a loose floor tile echoed over the cubicle partition. "You promised," Min called.

"I did no such thing," came Max's muffled reply. She must be squeezing into the crawlspace.

Min considered how to isolate commands by their targets, which distracted from her cringe over Max worming through a space designed for cabling. Min probed Bruce's custom command interface a bit more. Now she had a succinct list of relevant commands: "secure-lab," "notify-lab", "open-lab," "stop-lab," and "start-lab."

Min sighed, evaluating which one would unlock the interior door. She typed "open-lab" and hit the ENTER key.

The terminal blanked, and Min scrunched her eyes as the display erupted with characters. Row after row of gibberish ate up the blackness until a pattern emerged. It was a picture, each pixel made of a text character mimicking a shape. What the nerds called ASCII art. Fun to find on a normal day, but this one left a hollow in Min's gut.

It was a skull. It filled the screen, leaving space for a line of text at the bottom of the terminal: HELLO, MAX. NOW I KNOW WHERE YOU ARE, AND I'M COMING TO KILL YOU.

21

No Good Goose

Min hollered as she ran to the workspace door. "Max? Max?! I may have tripped a security protocol!"

No answer. Min found an open floor panel, leaned close to it. "Max? Can you hear me?"

A shuffling sound, then from the tight space Max asked, "Yeah, what's the problem?"

"I tried the obvious command, and it seems to have caused... something."

"Something?" Max's tone sounded stiff.

"I don't have details, except that it's not nice. And directed at you."

More rummaging echoed from the opening. "Seriously?"

"Yes!" Min replied. An unexpected noise slapped her ears. The clack of the hallway door slamming open. "Holy shit, Max, someone's here! Stay there, stay quiet," Min whispered into the crawlspace as she scooted the floor tile over the hole.

Before the tile clicked home, Max pleaded, "Take Bork and hide!"

Min spun on her haunches, looking for the dog. He wasn't here. She cursed under her breath, at the same time straining to pick up sounds, sense movement in the air. A series of dull thuds echoed; someone was stomping through the cubicle maze, closing in on her.

Min struggled to remember the layout, think of the best hiding spot. Then realized she had no time. A beam of light appeared, scanning over the partitions. Min scuttled backwards into a cubicle as the light rounded the near corner of the maze.

The approaching steps raced to a jog, and she clamped her hands over her mouth. The interloper stopped at the cube partition behind her.

A wheeze leaked from the stranger. Shadows drifted across the ceiling as the light steadied. The person was examining something. The locked door.

There was a jiggle of the door handle. Then a huff and a chuckle of satisfaction. A baritone buzzed in the dark. "Where are you hiding?"

Min recognized the voice: Bruce Gose.

Any comfort in the familiarity scattered when he started hollering. "Where are you, Max? I swear to God, if you give me what I want, I'll make it quick." The light pivoted over her hiding spot, a beacon of fear passing centimeters above her head. "You can't hide forever."

The silence of the room was so absolute that Min worried Bruce would detect her rattling nerves.

"Come out!" Bruce screamed, slamming the cube wall again. Min bit her lips closed to keep from yelping as dust cascaded into her eyes.

He doesn't realize you're here. Stay quiet, stay still.

There was a soft tap, just audible over her thrashing pulse: Bruce padding along the edge of the cube maze. "You remember Haoyu? From Materials? He's been bragging for months," he yelled. "Says he got past your fortress. Cornered you in the cafeteria. Bashed your head in." Min's eyes stayed locked on the shifting view of the hung ceiling tiles as his beacon scanned the room.

"I knew he was lying," Bruce spat, hammering the partition wall so hard Min flinched. "He would have taken something of yours to prove it. Maybe the collar of your stupid dog."

Dust particles flowed in the air, giving the searching light volume and weight as it sliced over her head once more.

"But no matter. I'm going to find you. You'll give me what I want, and I'm leaving this shit-hole of a world."

· • • ● • ● • • ·

Max wormed herself out of the floor, struggling to keep quiet. The muffle of Bruce's tirade suggested he wouldn't be able to detect anything quieter than an explosion from inside of this room. But he sounded pissed, so Max wasn't taking the chance.

She sat up, legs planted in the crawlspace, and took in Bruce's lab. Papers and wires cluttered the workbench across from her, and various electronic components lay scattered on the floor. Classic Bruce—she couldn't tell if someone trashed the place, or if this chaos was how he worked.

She crawled upright, cautious of rubble that might crunch or clatter under her boots. She dusted the crawlspace bunnies off her sweater, taking in the workspace proper.

The pale glow of a second terminal filled the room with pasty light. The screen displayed an ASCII art skull, along with a nasty note: HELLO, MAX. KNEW YOU COULDN'T STAY AWAY. NOW I KNOW WHERE YOU ARE, AND I'M COMING FOR YOU.

She shook her head, swallowed her disgust, and muttered, "Guess saving your life doesn't count much with you." She traced the power cable out of the terminal as it snaked behind a metal storage cabinet and sprouted through a grommet in Bruce's workbench.

It ended in what Max assumed was a power bottle. Not the cobbled bottle-and-bulb design they used this morning. This was a single cylinder, with no obvious compartment for the black hole or radiation containment. Max guessed the components were in there, concealed by the smooth metal chassis. A small glass LED inset by the power coupling reported the bottle's output and evaporation rate.

Another rattle came through the wall. Was Bruce throwing stuff? An image of Bork and Min cowering under a desk splashed into her mind. They had to get out of here. In a rush of adrenaline, Max clutched the bottle. She twisted the coupling a quarter-turn and disconnected the power source.

The terminal snapped to black, and the room disappeared in darkness. A tumble in her gut told Max she had made a huge mistake.

22

Well, Actually...

Min had her breathing under control, now that Bruce was searching the distant corridors of the cubicle farm. His rampage rattled the floor as he trashed something—tearing out a partition wall between cubes, maybe.

The noise's wake left a disconcerting silence. A sound was missing. A hum she only noticed once it was gone: the mild buzz of the terminal monitor.

She braved a glance up, not finding the feeble glow from the screen in the dark. Had Bruce turned it off? Smashed it?

No, she realized. It was Max. She had found the power source and disconnected it. Which meant-

"Ha!" Bruce shouted. "Now I know where you are!" Clomping footfalls approached, growing fierce as Bruce ran to his locked workspace.

A percussive slap marked Bruce hitting the door. It repeated several times before he spoke. "You know what that bottle was powering, Max? My terminals, sure. But actually-"

A horrifying sound drifted from the other side of the partition: the soft click of the door latch retracting.

"It also powered the lock on that room you're in, you impulsive dumbass!"

• • • • • • • • • •

His derisive words came as Max eased the floor tile over her face. The door pounded into the wall, and Bruce's stomps closed on her.

Sounds amplified in the narrow crawlspace. Max closed her eyes against the falling dust as the man stepped right over her. She wouldn't move - she couldn't without making noise, and it was impossible to wiggle fast enough through the crawlspace to ditch him. If he realized she was here, he'd open the floor and grab her before she could squirm off.

So, what then? Wait for him to lose interest and leave? Not a proactive strategy. Her brow knitted, and she cursed herself. It was impulsive of her to rip out the bottle. She hadn't thought through the consequences. Now she had to figure a way out of this hole. This lab. This awful situation. And then this disastrous future.

More sounds fell from above: the squeak of Bruce opening his storage cabinets, the stutter of workbenches sliding around. He was searching for her. Max opened her eyes, letting them dart over the tile millimeters from her nose. *How long until he tears up the floor?*

As if in response to the thought, the tile ripped aside and light blinded her.

• • • • • • • • • •

"Gotcha!" Bruce yelled, with a giddiness in his voice that left Min hollow and scared.

A muffled scream came from the room ahead. Min ran into the doorway, taking advantage of the commotion to move fast and close the distance to Bruce. He stooped, his flashlight casting long shadows as his arm disappeared into the crawlspace. Another yell shot from the hole under him as he heaved Max up by a fistful of her hair.

"Where is it?" Bruce spat as he worked the tiny woman out of the gap. "Where?!"

Max was on the floor now, rather than under it. She cowered prone as Bruce stood over her. His foot went to her lower back, and he shifted his weight to hold her there.

He hadn't noticed Min in the doorway yet. She had moments to act. Her gaze pulsed over the messy space for a weapon, sufficient to knock Bruce out without killing him. She saw papers, blueprints, and diagrams. Small electronic components and cables. A soldering iron that registered as useless because there was no chance it was hot.

She grabbed it anyway, clutching the gelled handle like a chef's knife, and lunged at Bruce. He turned right as she connected, the blunt tip glancing off of his shoulder and tearing his tattered lab coat.

"What the-!" he screamed, but there was no anger. Just shock. His arms flailed, and Min drove forward again before he could recover. Aiming for his shoulder, she stabbed the air. Something slammed into her arm, and she heard the soldering iron clatter into the surrounding mess. As he gained his bearings, Bruce's hand appeared in her periphery before it connected with her temple.

She staggered backwards and hit the floor. A white pain erupted on the left side of her head. Static consumed what little detail was present in the low light, and a coppery tang lit up her tongue.

Through the haze, an anger bubbled in her gut, and to her surprise it made a sound. A wet and rattling growl of concentrated frustration.

But the sound wasn't coming from her.

· · ● ● ● ● ● ● · ·

Max swiveled in time to watch Min splat on the floor, her head lulled to the side in a daze. From the doorway, a shadow skulked into the room.

Neils Bork, drawn out of hiding by the scuffle and Max's hollers. He let out a low moan, a warning that he wanted to know what was going on. Max smiled. She prayed that Future-Bork was as similar to Past-Bork as she needed him to be.

"Bork!" she called. The dog padded forward, eyebrows shifting as he took in the scene and people with tentative eyes. When the dog's stare locked on to hers, Max issued the command.

"*Mansplain!*"

The canine's demeanor flipped. Hackles raised, ears pinned, eyes darkened—his moan turned into a growl, and spit flew between his bared teeth.

"Woah, okay, wait!" Bruce stammered. He scurried away from Bork, stumbling between the storage cabinet and workbench.

The dog bounded at Bruce, jaws snapping at the air in front of him. Bruce made a racket as he staggered into the workbench, scattering papers and electronics across its top. His voice careened an octave as he squealed, "Dammit, hold up-"

The dog did as Max trained him to do: every time the man spoke, the dog barked and lunged, herding him from the women and not letting him speak or defend himself.

A second later, Bruce bolted out the workspace door, and Bork tore after him, nipping at his ankles. More shouts erupted from Bruce, along with more barking from Bork. The cacophony faded as the chase moved through the common room. Max eased herself up. As she helped Min to her feet, a single *whomp* sounded: the hallway door slamming against the wall. Bruce had run from the lab.

"Thank you," Min said. She touched her temple and winced at the tender welt. "What the hell was that all about? Why is he angry enough to hurt us?"

"I don't know."

From the doorway came the rhythmic taps of the dog's nails on the tile as he circled the cube farm, huffed through the maze, and checked for other dangers. Max fished the power bottle out of her cargo pants. "I found this. It was powering the terminals."

"Awesome. Let's see if there's anything else we can use." Min turned and dropped to grab Bruce's light off the ground. She moaned as she stood, her face clamping into a scowl as if holding in her brain. "I'm fine," she said before Max could ask. "Just going to have a headache for a while."

The light washed the darkness off of everything as the women rummaged through the room. Max cracked open the storage cabinet, finding two additional power bottles in an artifact box. She added hers, holding the box out for Min to see. "Why steal one black hole when you can steal two? Or three?"

Min's smile was brighter than the flashlight. "At least we solved the power problem. Can we use one of these to drive the Foresight control room?"

"Yes," Max confirmed. "We should head back."

Min shone the light across the workbench. "One sec, I want a weapon to defend ourselves if Future-Bruce shows up again." Nothing in the mess caught her interest.

"Past-Bruce kept a scepter behind that door," Max suggested. The "Magnetic Inversion Lock Facilitator" was a common tool at the institute. Everyone called it the "scepter" because of its shape and because the official acronym of the official name was officially offensive. Its design was little more than a standard basin plunger, with a magnet glued under the rubber dome. When you pressed the plunger against a floor tile, the magnet released the locks holding the tile down. Then the seal of the rubber allowed you to lift the tile. A valve on the handle would release the tile back into place. Not a weapon by design, but in a pinch, it might make a decent club.

Min shrugged and moved to the door. Behind it, her light revealed the scepter. She lifted it, testing its heft before resting it against her shoulder.

Max's gaze floated to the closing doorway as Bork arrived, sniffing the air to check on his people. The beacon splayed onto a poster on the back of the workspace door.

"What's that?" Max asked. She set her box on the workbench and closed the door to light more of the art.

It was a mock "wanted" poster with four mugshots arranged in a grid. As Min steadied the light, Max realized they were standard headshots, the kind every Daft Institute employee kept in their digital profile. Max recognized her own face, and Min's. Each photo hung above a caption, identifying them by name: MAX CANTROS and MIN DRAPER. In the second row of photos, she found Waffel's smirk, along with another person she didn't know. A long, lean face, with high cheekbones and broad eyes that radiated intelligence, framed with hair curly as Max's, but longer than Min's.

Min leaned closer, squinting at the name beneath the face. "Alice Courgette. Recognize her?"

"No. Never heard of her, either. You?"

Min shook her head, backing away and illuminating the poster's top, revealing words in an Old West typeface: WANTED, THE FOUR WHORES OF THE APOCALYPSE.

Max's heart landed in her stomach. She puffed out a frustrated breath. "Oh, come on!"

"For Pete's sake," Min sighed, "the end-of-times couldn't be the end-of-misogyny?" She shoved the door open with her sneaker, hiding the inflammatory poster and revealing Bork's proud dog grin in the doorway. "Let's get those data files and go home."

"Agreed," Max replied. The box of bottled singularities felt heavy as she swiped it up from the workbench. "Once we're home, remind me to kick Bruce in the nuts."

Min stepped into the common room, giving the patient Bork a love pat on her way through the door. "You'll have to get in line."

23

You Won't Believe #4!

Several sections of floor inside the Foresight control room lay open while Max traced the lab's power to its main coupling. While she did this, Min used the rover's tablet to recall BigWheels to the hallway in front of the lab. With the axels spread to maximize stability and the sensor arm pressed against the door's frame, BigWheels turned from intrepid explorer to squat guardian of the Foresight lab. Then she configured a new alarm: if the automaton detected movement, the tablet would notify them.

Right after Min tested the audible alert, the Foresight lab filled with light.

"There we go," Max sang. "We have power." The engineer nestled the connected power bottle into the crawlspace as she spoke. "Our terminals should work. Campus network is still offline, so we won't be able to access anything else." While Max cleaned up her cables, Min examined the illuminated room.

The intense LEDs dulled on the hazy layer of grime coating everything. The off-white paneling on the walls was filthy and greasy-looking. Min hadn't realized how much the air recyclers purified their environment.

She moved to her terminal. Its power switch snapped with a satisfying *clonk* and the screen came to life. While the operating system loaded, Min dusted off her chair and sat down. Max did the same, then crab-walked her seat to Min's side.

"Where should we start?" Min asked.

"We want all the laboratory logs since the day we left home," Max said. "May I?" She reached for the keyboard and started issuing complex shell commands Min wasn't familiar with. A wall of text cascaded down the display. "That's terabytes of files. It'll take days to copy using DOWN."

"A direct connection should speed things along. I think there's a LightWire in the cabinet. Or there was." Min stood and walked to the metal storage unit against the wall. The shelves should have contained a disorganized array of snacks—Min's jerky and granola, Max's ramen and potato crisps—as well as various electrical and system components, hand tools, and the cable they needed at this moment. It contained no food or tools, but a scattered assortment of random computer parts cluttered the shelves. Her heart skipped a beat. She saw no LightWire. In a beat of frustration, she rummaged through the shelves with her hands. On the narrow bottom shelf, where the women had stashed a change of clothes, Min found the connector she needed.

She returned to her terminal to find Max running a web browser. As she connected the tablet to her computer, she asked, "The network's unavailable. What are you hoping to see?"

Max's eyes were bright as she looked to Min. "True, but I want to snoop the browser cache. The local copy of everything Future-Min was poking through before..." She gestured a lazy hand at their surroundings.

Min melted into her chair as she chuckled, "Please don't judge me on what you find in there, okay?"

Max snorted, returning her gaze to the browser. "Honey, I've seen your dating profile already. Okay, I've sorted the cached files by date. The oldest was saved about nine months ago. The most recent is three months old. Or... six months in the future for us."

Min sighed. "Start at the newest and work our way back?"

"Seems like a plan. Before we do that, let's grab our logs." Max clattered on the keys again, sending reams of data files through the LightWire and into the tablet's local storage. Then, after resorting the browser cache, she opened the first file.

Min recognized the site: a news aggregation outlet she preferred. There was no article, however. Just a headline in a heavy and imperative typeface. "Pray for us all," she read aloud.

The words hung between the women. After a moment, Max sniffed the silence away. "Well, we already knew the ending, right?"

Min swallowed the fear thickening in her throat. "Yeah, true. Let's find out what happened."

"And why we're blamed for it," Max added.

They backtracked through the files, retracing their future history as pieces of the story percolated out of the cache. Most contained more articles, and the headlines were grave: TEN WAYS TO SPEND THE END OF DAYS; WHY I HATE DAFT AND EVERYONE WHO WORKS THERE; SEVEN HIDDEN BENEFITS OF FATAL X-RAY EXPOSURE; THREE TIPS FOR WINNING THE DIASPORA LOTTERY; PROTECTING YOUR SKIN DURING CORONAL MASS EJECTIONS.

Min put a hand on Max's shoulder to stop her from scrolling to the next article as a word caught her eye. "Look there," she pointed a finger at the screen and read aloud:

Dr. Shauna Waffel, COO and Chief Scientist for Daft Logistics, a wholly owned subsidiary of the Daft Institute, asserted that plans are underway to build transfer portals to migrate every person to a safe, off-world alternative.

"Transfer portals? Off-world?" Max parroted.

Min shook her head. "I don't understand either." She kept reading:

However, anonymous sources inside of Daft Logistics have said that neither the production methods nor materials exist to create that many portals in the time humanity has left. The United Nations released a public statement earlier today, expressing reluctance to work with Daft, citing the Institute's "lack of governance and safety as the cause of the very problem we now endure."

"Jesus," Max sighed.

Min felt the prickling nerves carried on her friend's voice. Frustrated, she skimmed the rest of the page. "There," she placed a fingertip on the purple link in the article's sidebar: THIS IS HOW THE WORLD ENDS. "Click on that."

24

EDITING HISTORY

Max clicked the dire text. A video opened on-screen. The women relaxed into their chairs as a date faded from black: August 24, 2019. Almost five years in their past. The crisp text dissolved as an image took its place. Dr. Waffel standing in the center of a large aperture, smiling with pride. Min and Max flanked her, along with a third woman Min recognized as Alice Courgette.

"Wait a minute," Max whispered. "Do you remember taking that photo? Because I don't."

Min opened her mouth, but her words failed as the video's baritone narration kicked in.

The Daft Institute pioneered the field of quantum displacement in 2022, under the direction of Dr. Shauna Waffel. Working from theories of dimensional folding proposed by Dr. Alice Courgette, the Institute performed the first successful test of a transfer portal in 2023.

Min's brow ached with confusion. "None of that is true, though."

Max's shoulders shrugged, just in Min's periphery. Min turned to face her friend. "Would you put it past Waffel to rewrite history to make herself look better?" At the sound of Max's voice, Bork shuffled to sitting in his bed by her side, resting his chin on her thigh. Without taking her gaze from the video, Max massaged the dog's ears and neck. "What the heck is 'quantum displacement' and 'dimensional folding'? I've never heard you use those terms."

"I don't know," Min admitted. As if hearing her, the narrator explained.

A Daft-patented technology, the Transfer Portal creates a stable wormhole by folding higher spatial dimensions. This allows people and materials to be transported over vast distances with minimal physical travel.

A familiar scene filled the screen—a forward view of the aperture, with those strange concentric phosphorescent halos radiating out to the chrome ring. After a few moments, the light show calmed to an alien landscape, framed by the round aperture. A rugged horizon, all rocks and rust-hued sand.

"Is that... Mars?" Min asked.

Max remained silent, engrossed in the video of a BigWheels rolling up a ramp, through the aperture, and then rocketing over the scrabbled Martian ground. The mottled red dust that seeped through the portal was stark against the blazing white surfaces of the surrounding clean room.

Min's tablet chimed. A notification from the rover guarding the lab door. She glanced at the tablet to verify nothing was moving in the hallway.

"We safe?" Max asked. She had paused the video, and her saucer eyes probed Min.

Min nodded. "Yeah, just another ping from the radiological sensors on the BigWheels. Normal background stuff. It isn't dangerous."

The engineer's body melted a bit, and she took a moment to exhale her tension. "That's not our lab," she said, gesturing to the video. "The room is too large. And it looks like an airlock has been built around the aperture. Have you ever seen that before?"

"Never."

Max nodded, sighed again as she resumed the video.

The image shifted to an orbital view of the Earth—a curved azure horizon against a black sky. The frame shook. After a few seconds, the planet rotated out of view. A sea of stars emerged as the camera's AI adjusted for the low contrast.

Daft monetized the technology, creating the Daft Logistics shell corporation with the single and ambitious goal of mining asteroids. This video, taken by Cosmonaut Kemper from the cupola of the International Space Station, shows the construction of Orbital Transfer One.

The video tracked to a speck in the window. As the image clarified, a shape congealed. A wide, round arc floating in space. Motion became apparent on the oblique surface: insectile fabrication robots scuttling across the structure.

With a diameter of eight kilometers, OTO was large enough to allow the passage to and from the surface of asteroids for fleets of mining automatons.

A diagram appeared. A blueprint of the OTO. Min noted the core design of the ring that brought her and Max to this horrid future: a round frame of exotic metal, its iridescent sheen visible between the fibers of vanadium dioxide; hanging off the aperture ring was a pill-shaped enclosure. Without knowing the scale of the schematic, Min assumed it was a power bottle.

Because of the immense energy requirements of the transfer portal, OTO required a novel power source. Something capable of generating more energy than humans had seen to date. The Zero Point Module (in the diagram, a red highlight surrounded the pill attached to the ring) is a scaled-up version of the standard artificial singularity module that provides power to your own home.

Shauna Waffel's saccharine smile appeared. Her marketing face, the one she used when talking to the public or her superiors.

Of course it's safe, Video-Waffel said. *It's proven technology we use daily. These power modules have never breached their containers, and there's every indication they will scale up to the levels required. Plus, we've added measures to ensure public trust in this. If the singularity in the ZPM breaches containment, it will launch on a trajectory that carries it out of the solar system, long before the black hole can consume enough matter to sustain itself.*

The diagram reappeared. A frowny-face emoji decorated the pill-shape. The ZPM disconnected from the aperture and zoomed away. As it departed, the emoji's expression morphed to a barfy-face. Then the pill disappeared from existence with a stylized, animated *pop*.

So there's no reason to worry, Video-Waffel concluded.

"Famous last words," Max mumbled.

Min had to agree. This was leading to something catastrophic.

The screen faded to black. Then another date crept out of the darkness: February 11, 2026.

Min swallowed. "About six months into the future. Our future."

Dread swelled as the subtitle appeared: CATACLYSM.

25

CΛTΛCLΥSM

The video transitioned to a control center, dozens of workstations arranged in auditorium seating that circled an immense display. Several smaller areas of the wall screen displayed telemetry Min didn't recognize. The rest contained a familiar sight: the head-on view of an aperture.

With nothing to offer scale, it could have been a microscopic aperture from the original Foresight design. However, the array of stars glinting in the portal conveyed the immensity of this object. This was OTO, the kilometers-wide aperture above the Earth.

The heads in front of each workstation pivoted, operators exuding professional calm as they monitored the instrumentation from the monstrosity in space. The feed was silent until a male voice punched through the speakers.

All stations, this is Mission Control. I need your final go, no-go for portal initiation. All stations must report in.

The right side of the wall display flipped to a checklist. Min guessed at some of the unreadable labels: power, communications, network, security. Over several moments, green checkmarks popped up next to each item.

All stations have acknowledged ready status. Prepare for portal initiation. Count down sixty seconds on my mark. Mark!

A 60-second timer appeared beneath the checklist and began cycling down. The women waited, breath bated as each tick of the timer closed on an unknown dread.

With ten seconds left, the male voice spoke. *Power, prepare to open the coupling, confirm the draw is seventeen petawatts.*

Max gagged upon hearing the number, and Min's chilly apprehension gave way to a warming awe. It was an inconceivable amount of energy.

Five... four... three... two... one... Power, open the coupling.

A white brilliance filled the control room, and Min squinted. The blaze vanished, revealing the spirals of light inside the OTO. They rippled outward, the curved arcs thinning and multiplying until the entire center was awash in a yellow glow.

In a blink, it snapped to black. The aperture contained a starless void, darker than the surrounding space.

Power, confirm energy transfer.

Control, Power. Confirming seventeen petawatts of continuous energy transfer into the portal. An unfamiliar voice. Younger, but just as collected and blase as the mission controller.

A moment of quiet passed as more of the operators raised their gaze to the large, dark hole framed in gleaming chrome.

A woman's voice filled the strangling silence.

Control, Image Intel. Movement detected within the OTO.

IMINT, confirm you said 'movement'?

Before the woman could answer, the OTO disappeared from the screen. The emptiness inside the aperture exploded out. The image details were sparse but enough to convey an immense blackness pouring into the surrounding space, obscuring the ring and stars.

IMINT, report! The male voice again, tense with concern.

Operators began to stand and gawk.

Control, Image Intel. We've lost visuals from the satellites.

Control, Comms. A fresh voice came to the mix, carrying an edge of panic. *Confirm signal loss from the monitoring satellites.*

Cries on the video swelled, a clatter of station reports and responses scrambling to be heard as mission control pleaded for protocol.

The view shifted to OTO as seen from the ISS. A mass of dark tentacles roiled out of the aperture, shuddering the ring with their force. Zoomed in, the quality of the video was clear enough to show the black alien fingers—an uncountable number of them, spilling out of the aperture faster than eyes could follow. Some clutched the ring itself, buckling the woven coil. Others shot ahead and, after a few moments of breakneck descent, slammed into the Earth in a fury of smoke and dust.

Through the cacophony of voices, one terrified scream stood out: *Control, Telemetry! Seismic sensors are pegged! We have an earthquake of unknown magnitude!*

Panic sweat tickled Min's spine as those other-worldly tendrils streamed out of the portal and tore visible gouges into the planet's surface. As more wormed into the ground, the Earth dulled. After mere moments, there was more brown haze than green land or blue ocean as particulates saturated the atmosphere.

Audio cut out. The milieu of terror severed mid-screams. A disturbing silence accompanied the flood of destruction, and Min held her breath. The scratches on the planet expanded to canyons, and the opaque cloud concealing the impact site exploded a sickening shade of orange.

"My God," Max cried. "It's cracking the planet in half!"

Fourteen seconds after initiation, OTO failed, the original narrator reported. *The transfer portal buckled, collapsing the wormhole and blocking the attacking force. But the damage was done. The event threw enough dust into the atmosphere to create a nuclear winter that scientists (unaffiliated with the Daft Institute) predict will last for years. Of more pressing concern-*

The video homed in to the ZPM. A dark fissure had appeared in its smooth white surface, and waves of chaff spun around the oblong capsule before zipping into the small gap. Min's chest tightened as the video confirmed her fears.

-was the breach of the Zero Point Module containment. As mentioned by Dr. Waffel, precautions were in place to expel the black hole from the solar system.

Another diagram appeared. Planets orbiting the sun, concentric rings circling a single point that reminded Min of the ripples of light in the apertures. A line emerged, starting at the third planet. The orbital model rotated to show the intended trajectory of the ZPM leading out of the planetary plane.

Unfortunately, the catastrophic incident changed the OTO's orientation in space, and with OTO Mission Control destroyed, there was no way to correct this before the automated launch systems took control.

The diagram adjusted. The ZPM's projected path rotated, easing into the plane of the orbiting planets. Min willed it to stop; she wanted to reach into the screen and hold it back. But the line settled, and both women sucked in a gasp as Min's hand landed over her gaping mouth.

The ejection path intersected with the sun.

Max cried a miserable sound. She pulled her short legs up to her chest, lowered her head, and curled into a ball. "I can't watch anymore of this."

"I get it." Min reached around her friend to tap the spacebar on the keyboard, pausing the video. "We need to know, though. The more information we can bring back with us, the better our chances of preventing this from happening."

Max pushed against the desk, spinning her chair and getting to her feet. Neils Bork stood, obedient eyes locked on his human as she paced by him. "We'll be in the clean room. I need to stare at our past for a minute and pet my dog. Pull your data, Min. Then let's get the hell out of this place. Or time. Or whatever. I just want to go home."

26

Gravity Well, Actually

A red tinge tamped the light streaming out of the portal. Max wasn't sure why; Min could probably explain it, and Max would ask her before they went home if she thought of it. For now, the odd color was giving Neils Bork's fur a ruddy glow, a magical visual effect that suggested that if this was one of the adventure games she loved to play, the dog had her next side quest.

If only this were a game. Billions dead in seconds. The remaining survivors doomed to a slow, freezing death as the singularity consumed the sun. And the world blamed the four women.

They may have worked on the technology, but they never controlled its application. If anyone was at fault, it was Waffel. That conniving woman would sell her own mother if it suited her needs, and she would certainly cut corners if it greased the Machiavellian gears of Daft's management career track.

And why had Bruce dumped the blame on her and Min? It was his ZPM that would end up killing everyone, not Foresight.

Quick abstractions lead to ugly reactions. Hanlon's Razor. Max didn't want to presume ill intent where stupidity provided an adequate explanation, but she would not be culpable for the world's destruction. Seated on the floor, she buried her face into the dog's neck to clear her mind. His pinching dander filled her nose. "Bork, I love you. And you need a bath."

Her breath tickled Bork's ear, which twitched against her cheek in response. Max rubbed her fingers into the soft cartilage and massaged the itch away as the dog licked her chin.

A flash of purple caught her eye. She unfolded his dangling ear flap to get a better peek, finding a tattoo on the hairless underside of his ear. This was unique—the first sign that this dog differed from the Bork she had lost. She read the blocky letters to herself. "Bork MK-2. What is that? Bork Mark 2?"

Max realized the implications of the marking. Daft had long pursued cloning programs, and rumors had circulated that the Institute had shirked the global ban on human cloning. She took the dog's cheeks in her hands, framed his snout to her nose. "Are you a clone? Are you my beautiful, good, clone boy?"

His eyes shifted from Max to the rusty light spilling through the portal, his eyebrow tilts giving him an anthropomorphic expression of dire concern. Max kissed his wet, rubbery dog lips before letting go of his smooshed fur.

The clean room door clattered open, and Max returned to her feet as Min traversed the doorway.

"Please tell me you're ready to leave?" Max begged.

Min nodded. "Yeah, we need to leave. I found orbital models on Future-Min's computer. Predictions and best-guesses at how long Earth has to exist."

"And time's up, I'm guessing?"

"Overdue. I think that's why the sky looks so strange. The black hole ended up in an elliptical orbit around the sun. At each perigee, it's tearing off wads of stellar mass. It's consuming most of it, and yeeting the leftovers into space. And look at this—remember those notifications from the BigWheels?"

Min shoved the control tablet in front of her and pointed at the stream of alerts. A stack of red notification boxes, each containing the same text: WARNING: HAWKING RADIATION DETECTED.

"Um, are we being irradiated?" Max felt her throat tighten.

"No. Hawking radiation isn't the danger. It's a marker, because it only occurs near a black hole."

Max looked at the notifications again. "So the singularity survived? And is heading towards Earth?"

Min's emphatic nod caused a few strands of hair to fall across her face. "And we don't want to be here when it gets close. We may already be experiencing its effects, and they'll only get worse. Time dilation, seismic shifts, stuff like that."

Three rising, shrill chimes whistled from the tablet in Min's hands.

"More radiation alerts?"

Min's free hand returned the loose hair back behind her ear as her brow furrowed. "No, I silenced those." Max scooted close to the woman's shoulder, watching the glowing display as Min tapped her way to the tablet's primary screen.

A flashing red box pulled her attention to the evaporation timer—the countdown until dissipation of the singularity that was feeding their open portal home. Before they crossed the aperture, it had read five years.

What it reported now made Max's heart stop.

Ten seconds.

• • • ● • ● • • •

Max was yelling. Gathering the dog. Pulling on Min.

But Min couldn't speak, frozen as the readout flipped to zero in a blink.

Her gaze slipped from the tablet to the decaying visage of their home laboratory. It was bright and white when they arrived, just hours ago. Now a deep red hue stained everything on the other side of the aperture.

A logic train hooked up in her head: the approaching singularity, the time dilation caused by immense gravity, and how years back home would pass in hours if this Earth was far enough in the gravity well of the black hole.

The scarlet light darkened to crimson. The circular tear in the air lost its crisp edge.

Then their home disappeared.

27

THIRST TRAP

"What the hell?" Max's hand scratched the empty air, as if she could pry open the past with her fingers. "Fucking Bruce! That power bottle was supposed to last for five years! It's only been three hours!"

Min remained stone. As the implications clarified, her tablet fell from her hands. In response, an agitated Bork scuttled into the corner. It was his shaking that pulled Min out of her stupor.

"Time dilation," she whispered.

Max turned, her eyes bouncing in their sockets before they found Min. "What did you say?"

"Time dilation," she repeated, recovering her voice. "Gravity bends space, and it slows time. They're linked. I think the singularity is slowing time for us."

Max's petrified stare bobbed. Her fingers clenched her scalp. "So while we were putzing around here, dealing with Bruce's bullshit-"

"Five years must have passed at home. The power bottle evaporated."

Max's palms slapped her sides, startling Min and the dog. "Oh! Perfect! So what now?" she hollered. "How do we get back? And how am I supposed to explain a five-year gap in my resume?"

Bork cried out at his human's frustration, and Min flinched into the wall. The net impact on Max was immediate. Her chest heaved, eyes dewy as she collapsed and wept. Min slid down, the paneling's flange scraping her back until she hit the floor.

After a few breaths, Bork approached Max. He leaned into her, his snout nestling into her neck. Her arms moved around him as she asked, "What do we do, Min?"

"We can't stay here, Max. There aren't any positive aspects to being close to a sustained black hole. The longer we wait, the more danger we're in."

After another breath, Max replied, "I want to go home."

"Me too. Bork is on board with that, I'm certain. But we need a functioning aperture. We have the power bottles to make it work," she said, her gaze flitting to the wall and the control room beyond. "Maybe we repeat what we did to get here, and it gets us home?"

"You don't sound sure."

"I'm not," she admitted. "Not in the least. I'm guessing. I don't even know if it's an educated one or not, but it's all I can think of."

Max nodded, her face disappearing into the dog's extra neck skin. She reappeared, sniffling back her running nose. "In that video, Daft was using apertures for all sorts of stuff. There's got to be some in the building. We need to find them."

"We shouldn't split up," Min said. "Bruce is out there."

"We could send the BigWheels," Max offered, her demeanor perking up now that they were working on a problem. "Reprogram the AI with new search criteria."

Min tilted her head, resting it against the paneling as she closed her eyes to the gleaming LEDs in the ceiling. "Yeah. We lose our safety barricade, though."

"We can hole up in the cafeteria. Someone secured every entrance. I had to crawl through the floor to get in."

Min considered it. "Will Bork and I be able to get in, too?"

"He could, with a little help from me. Your tall ass *might* fit."

The backhanded compliment caused Min to smirk, and she realized how tired she was. Her emotions drained, her physical will spent, yet their struggle continued to press on her. Max's levity was a gift in that moment, a drop into Min's empty spiritual cup.

She gathered the rover control tablet, using her foot to pull it within reach of her hands. "Alright then, I'll set up the new-"

A notification chime interrupted her, and an alert box appeared over the interface: Motion Detected.

"Now what?" Max sighed, exasperated. "Jury duty?"

Min tapped the alert to bring up the live video from the rover. The composite 360 view was difficult to parse. The long corridors and branching turns outside the lab stitched together like a Mobius helix. Thankfully, the AI highlighted the triggering movement with a yellow box and attached a label: HUMAN. The figure plodded forward. Inching towards the lab. Framed in the canary box was the unmistakable scowl and stringy beard of Dr. Bruce Gose.

"Dammit, it's Bruce again."

A flash of motion crossed the screen. Before Min or the AI could process what was happening, the telemetry disappeared. Bork let out a sharp yelp and pressed into Max.

"Shit. Shit! Something happened to the feeds."

"Let me see." Max scooted close enough to look at the tablet, then took it from Min and started tapping through the interface. "Sensors are out. Hell, even the hardened systems aren't responding."

A bright squeal caused the three of them to flinch. The cry of bending metal, but then Min recognized the noise for what it was: feedback from an amplified microphone.

"That was an electromagnetic grenade." Bruce's voice resonated through the door. "Harmless to you, but not so much to your Big-Wheels. This next one, though? You're going to feel it."

Min's gaze shot to Max. The engineer's stare widened as a dull *clank* hit the lab's door. Min's mind analyzed that sound—the decisive report of a magnet hitting metal—as Max tackled her and Bork into the wall.

A concussive blast pressed them close. Unbearable pressure crushed her body, and her ears registered a crackling scream that, even muffled through the mass of Bork and Max, surpassed her ear's ability to take it in.

Min unstuffed herself from her friends. She peered over the lip of the window into the control room. The main door to their lab had buckled out of its frame, and a creepy, pulsing light crawled into the room—a slow-seething viridescent fire that bubbled across the walls and ceiling, with flames the ominous green glow of the rover's nightvision. Except this was no computer-enhanced visualization. This was reality.

Her mouth dried up. Skin stiffened on her muscles. Air ripped from her lungs. Fear of dying in the explosion forgotten as every cell in her body screamed for the same thing.

Water.

As fast as it spread, the green flames and pressure dissipated. Yet her bottomless thirst surged.

Max. Was she okay? Min turned to check, discovering her prone, face to the ceiling, with her tongue swelling out of her mouth. Bork lay with her, slumped against the wall at an unnatural angle. Min tried to ask if they were alive, but her own tongue refused to get out of the way of the words.

Grey static eroded the edge of her sight. Then, like the dying portal she saw moments ago, darkness consumed everything.

28

Bargain

A rush of relief washed through Max's body. The quench of countless mouths sucking up oceans of water.

She gasped, her breath burning, but nothing near the pain she experienced after the explosion. A few seconds later, her pulse slammed against her skull hard enough to create stars in her vision.

"Those hydrobaric grenades are heinous, aren't they?"

Bruce's voice. Max opened her eyes, found him close. Face next to hers, his gaze lowered. She sat propped against the wall, her body tingling and heavy with weakness.

"I was forty meters away when it went off, and I felt it. Nasty weapon. Consumes moisture, dessicates living tissue. Experimental Daft technology and borderline war crime. Never would have seen the light of day, even if you bitches hadn't destroyed the Earth."

Max noted a pressure on her forearm. Her eyes rocked down to find a syringe being removed from her vein. Panic set in after a moment.

"What are you doing?" Her speech was sticky. Lungs clamped into fists.

"Giving you an electrolyte solution to help counteract the effects of the explosive." A rough hand gripped her cheeks, forcing her gaze up. "I'm content to let you die. Honestly, I'd buy a ticket to watch it happen. But you have something I need."

He released her with a shove, bouncing her throbbing head against the wall that triggered a fresh wave of nausea.

"So, where's the passkey?" he asked.

She heard the words. Sought to make sense of them. Blinking between brain-throbs, her gaze dropping to the parallel lines of the floor tiling. She followed them, and found Min and Bork piled across the room like battered rag dolls.

Max wanted to point. Her hands refused to work. She gestured with her chin. "Are they okay?"

"No." Bruce was back on his haunches now, rifling through a canvas bag. He held up another syringe, full of a viscous fluid the shade of shallow ocean water. "Give me the passkey, and I'll rehydrate them."

Her mind struggled with the ask, scouring for something to offer him. Leverage with which she could save Bork and Min. "What passkey? What the hell are you talking about?"

His beard narrowed as his expression soured. "Don't insult me. I know Waffel entrusted you with it."

She shook her head, fresh pain wracking her face. "Waffel's dead."

"Of course she is. She took the easy way out. And good riddance to her," he chuckled. "Her ambition ended the world. And you other bitches enabled her. You deserve to die. But not me. It wasn't my fault your portal summoned that thing that tore into the planet."

His aggression sparked a fire in her chest—a pilot light that ignited her senses. The flashes and sparkles in her sight cleared, and the lingering odors of copper and sulfur from the Bruce's weapon scrubbed the haze from her mind.

"So where is it?" he repeated.

She rocked her head again, tried to reach up to massage her temple. Bruce had secured her wrists with a few cable ties. Too many to break by force without cracking her bones. "I don't know, Bruce."

He wiggled the needle in his fingers, nodded toward the unconscious woman on the floor. "Time's wasting, Max. They only have a minute before hypovolemic shock sets in. Then there's nothing we can do except enjoy the show."

"I have no idea!" she huffed.

"Bullshit, Max." His voice fell, disappointment washing out his anger. The syringe disappeared into his bag, and his hand returned holding a computer tablet. After a few taps, he turned the small screen to her.

It was a still image from internal building sensors. Waffel and Max stood in front of a large aperture, at least eight meters tall. Waffel was laying a lanyard around Max's neck. Bruce's thin fingers spread the picture, zooming in on the rectangular device attached to the cord. Max hadn't realized what it was; however, she had seen it earlier that day.

"That's the passkey." His fingers pinched, zooming the photo back out. "That's Waffel placing it over your head. You have the only way into the transfer portal rooms, Max. And I WANT IT!"

Her mental fog at bay, disparate thoughts connected like jigsaw pieces. A clarity emerged that she'd lost during the confusion and chaos. She had encountered that rectangle ceramic casing earlier. She could get to it, and Bruce couldn't. And now Bruce confirmed that a working aperture was nearby.

"Okay," she sighed. "Okay. You win, Bruce. The passkey isn't here. Even if I told you where it was, you wouldn't be able to retrieve it. Only I can do that."

Bruce shrugged. "So let's go."

Her jaw clenched, chin lifted as she met his stare with defiance. "Not until you save my friends."

29

Heart Stompers

With Bork limping at her side and Min crutched on her shoulder, Max trudged towards the cafeteria. The dehydrating blast had incapacitated Min. While the electrolyte injection allowed her to function, she could not yet carry her full weight. The dog kept pace, but Max had never seen him this wrung-out.

And she was in no better shape. A sticky film reappeared in her mouth as quickly as she swallowed it back. It didn't help that Min's tall frame was leaning into her for support, a hand wrapped into the shoulder strap of the makeshift explosive vest Bruce had strapped to Max's torso.

"This is another hydrobaric grenade," Bruce had said as he fitted the bandoleer snug to her chest. "Rigged to my tablet. I'll be following at a safe distance. You leave my line of sight? Break into a run? Sick your damned mutt on me? Hell, if you even stop to tie your laces, I'll turn the three of you into powder."

One tedious step at a time, Max led the group through the halls. When she reached the barricade, she helped Min to the floor, and prompted Bork to lie beside her. Turning to Bruce, trailing them 30 meters away, she yelled, "The passkey is in the cafeteria. I have to crawl under this barrier."

The man offered a diminutive shrug. "Go on, then."

"Bruce, my body barely fits in the cable run. I can't get through with this contraption on me," she said, thumbing at the bomb on her sternum. "I need to take it off."

There was a prolonged silence as she watched Bruce play out scenarios like chess moves. At length, he motioned at her with the tablet in his hand. "Remove it, and put it on Minerva. If you're not back in five minutes with the key, your dog and friend are dust."

Max didn't waste time arguing. She unclipped the buckle holding the sling on her torso, relieved that the deadly weapon was no longer in contact with her body. She settled the bomb vest on Min's lap. From the cargo pocket on her calf, she removed the two power bottles and set them on the floor.

Max stooped to offer a few words to her friend. "I'll be back soon, Min. Don't worry. Okay?"

Min's chapped and bleeding lips didn't move; her eyes eased closed as she nodded.

"Timer's running, Max." Bruce kicked the polymer wall paneling twice for effect.

Max ran a quick hand over her dog's ears. Bork whined with exhaustion as Max pulled away and stood. She turned to the other wall, tapping floor tiles with her boot until she found one that shifted under the force. She dropped to her knees, spit on her palm, and slapped the smooth floor. Moving her hand in a few tiny circles, the vacuum bubble sucked against her skin, and she lifted.

The tile popped up. Max dove into the crawlspace head-first. She caterpillared her body into the tunnel, shifting her breath into her gut when she needed to squeeze around a fixed conduit. Bit by bit, she shimmied along, using her shoulders and feet, and counted her laborious progress by checking for loose tiles. After an eternity, one yielded to pressure.

She rushed herself out of the floor with uncoordinated twists and frustrated grunts. Then she rose, dusted herself off, and then hollered through the barrier, "I'm here! Fetching the passkey now!"

There was no response, and she chided herself for expecting one. She trotted from the pile of spot-welded industrial furniture and entered the broad seating area.

She remembered the space was empty, the tables and chairs used to build the protective barricades. Without her light, the room had turned liminal. Barren except for dangers hovering beyond the edge of her sight. A dismal rusty glow seeped out of a few circular areas in the ceiling. She hadn't noticed it earlier. Light pipes shuttling the dim radiance of the strange atmosphere into this room. At home, the translucent ceiling tiles shone on bright sunny days; even under an overcast sky, they provided some natural illumination inside of the subterranean building. These pipes emitted enough lumens of dirty orange to show the floor under her feet. The hallways leading off from the expanse remained black cutouts.

Max struggled to recall which corridor contained the dead body. She knew it was in this wing of the cafeteria.

As she checked the first one, another detail sprang from her memory: the hallway had been very dark, even with her tablet light. She hadn't seen the body until she was right on top of it. The tangerine haze behind her allowed her to see most of the way down this hall, to a glint of metal marking another barricade. She backtracked, trudging the edge of the main eating area for a passage dank enough to be a candidate.

There was only one—a single corridor positioned in the shadow created by a ten-meter gap in the glow. She advanced into the darkness, counting her steps to maintain her calm. The faint saccharine odor of death let her know she was in the right hallway.

Was the corpse on her left, or her right? She struggled to remember. Tried to recall the interaction with Bork. She mimed how she might turn around to admonish the dog, then rotate back and find the body.

On the left. Her hands raised, she eased toward the wall until she felt the cool paneling under her fingertips. Then she stooped, sliding one hand along the paneling, the other on the floor, inching forward at a delicate pace. She didn't want to plow into the corpse, or land her hands in the gore waiting in the dark.

Her right hand touched rubber. The fingers explored the object. It was the sole of a work boot.

A shudder passed through Max, so strong she had to sit. The shape under her fingertip was unmistakable. It was familiar to her. A heart-shaped cleat. There would be more arranged in a daisy pattern. Her fingertips drifted, confirming what she expected.

Her other hand moved to her own boot, verifying the same arrangement of heart-cleats: the boots on the corpse were Max's boots. A visage of Min came to mind, counting off tests to disprove what Max knew to be true.

This corpse was Future Maxine Cantros. Officially deceased and violently murdered.

Max had not examined the body before. Instead, she had bolted away. It wasn't until Bruce mentioned Haoyu's gloating over killing Future-Max in the cafeteria that she considered the possibility.

Not a mere possibility: Max was positive, now. This corpse was her. If she returned home, changed nothing, then this was how she would die.

A rumble came through the walls. It rattled away from her, into the building's higher stories. Min's words echoed in that guttural sound—the black hole was approaching the planet. If Max didn't get moving, she would perish twice in this horrific future.

Her hands hesitated on the legs of the corpse. Eased to the waist where her fingers spread to locate her objective: the item she saw in passing without realizing its significance. Her hand wrapped around a smooth, oblong ceramic rectangle, maybe 10 centimeters long, attached to a corded lanyard.

The passkey.

Max's fingers traced the lanyard to a small carabiner secured around her corpse's belt loop. She disconnected the thumb snap. Murmured an apology to her dead self. She stood and jogged into the dismal cafeteria as the building groaned again.

30

Silent Warning

Max squirmed her torso out of the crawlspace and sat on the edge of the floor tile, her feet still in the crawlspace. Min was standing now, with Bork still as a statue at her side. The physicist was wearing the bomb-laden bandoleer on her own torso now, the power bottles nestled in the crook of her elbow.

"You ok?" Max asked.

"I should ask you the same question," Min smiled.

Before Max could stand, Bruce called from down the hall. "The passkey?"

She rifled into her calf pocket, pulling out the fob and dangling it by the lanyard for Bruce to see. For several moments, she waited, sitting on the edge of the hole with her feet in the crawlspace. Bruce fiddled with his tablet, and Max realized he was using the camera to zoom. She choked up on the cord to stop the passkey's pendulum drift.

"That's it," he said. "Now, stand up."

Max stood, rising out of the crawlspace hole while taking a survey of Min and Bork. Mere hours in this dismal future had left them ragged. Scratches marred Min's drawn face, her lips split from dehydration. The dog, having recuperated from hunger, now hunched under a yoke of fear.

She took the power bottles from Min, replacing them back in the cargo pocket on her thigh.

"All of you walk my direction. Don't run, don't veer off course, or you know what happens."

They padded down the hall, Min walking on her own but using the wall for support. As they moved, Bruce paced away from them, keeping a safe distance.

After leading them through several intersections, Bruce held up a palm. "Drop the passkey, then back-step toward the cafeteria. Same rules as before."

Max made a dramatic show of setting the fob on the floor, then backed off several meters. Min's fingers brushed her forearm. Max turned, and the women shuffled away.

"Bruce knows where we can find working apertures," Max whispered. "He needs that passkey to get physical access to them."

Min squeezed her shoulder in acknowledgment.

"We need to get that vest off of you," Max continued. "Follow Bruce to the apertures. Then juice one up and go home."

Another squeeze, painful and sharp. Max glanced up and found Min's eyes wide. They locked with Max's stare for a protracted second, then fell with intent to the vest clenching her torso.

Hardware covered the bandoleer. Max hadn't noticed earlier, the bomb consuming her attention. A camera. Sensors she didn't recognize. And a microphone.

Shit!

Min had tried to warn Max—the squeeze wasn't an *ok-thank-you*, it was a *shut-the-hell-up-he-can-hear-you*.

"You're not going anywhere," Bruce called. "I'm taking the portal off-world to find the others. But you two aren't. You'll remain here and get torn to pieces with the planet."

The man's tone agitated the dog, who lowered his snout and tail with a whine. Max rubbed his cheek, set her hand under his chin to lift his gaze to hers. "Don't worry, I won't let that happen, Neils Bork."

"Stop there," Bruce hollered. "Use the staircase. Head down to Quantum Logistics. I'll follow a few floors above you. Consider your ass nuked if you misbehave, you hear me?"

Min reached the stairwell first. She pushed the door inward, the sound reverberating up and down the concrete spiral. Max ushered the dog ahead, then followed. As the door slid closed, Min's grip returned to her shoulder.

"He's using the DOWN," she whispered. Max struggled to uncover the context behind Min's words. It wasn't until she noted Min's other hand fisted around the microphone that Max understood.

"It's the only way he could pass information between devices without the primary network," she continued. "Take my tablet out of my back pocket, Max. Find the file he's using to proxy commands from his tablet to this vest."

Max understood what Min was thinking. The DOWN was a file-based network, designed for small amounts of slow communication rather than high-volume automation interfaces or operational controls. That didn't stop folks from using it to hack solutions to everyday problems. Such as the chat software they had cobbled together earlier.

"Quick!" Min pressed. "Before he comes into the stairwell and sees you!"

Max jerked the tablet from the rear pocket of Min's jeans, unlocking the screen before the clatter of the door shook the surrounding air. Bork shot to the next landing, shaking, while Max dropped the tablet to her thigh.

"It's okay Bork," Min sang. Min had uncovered the microphone, then skipped ahead one step. Enough that the front-facing camera wouldn't capture Max's actions. Max studied the vest again.

It had to be from the defense labs. A standard tactical vest with hard points for attaching gear. Max remembered the camera and microphone on the front, along with some kind of sensor array. On the shoulder, she found a wireless communications module.

You could just rip off the transmitter, Max thought. That would sever the connection to the DOWN. The idea landed in the do-not-try pile. Bruce had experience as an electrical engineer, and he was clever. It was a safe assumption that the bomb would trigger if she messed with the components.

No. If Max was to save them, she had to use Bruce's faults against him. In her mind, she rifled through her past interactions with the man: his dismissive manner in how he had approached Max to fix his fabrication programs; his smug reaction when she saved his life by sacrificing her beloved dog; the recent conversations in his workshop—one from the past, where he was so sure he had a safe solution to their power needs, and from this awful future, where he blamed the Armageddon created from his power system design on everybody else.

Not everybody. On her. On Min. On Dr. Waffel and this Alice person.

Bruce's weakness was *arrogance.* He believed that anything he touched was infallible and perfect and could not fail. That he was smarter than anyone. He had a specific disdain for women, especially those who challenged his intellect. Max hoped this aspect of his personality would create an opening to save Min, Bork, and herself.

31

Concrete Spiral

"Which floor are we shooting for?" Min's voice echoed against the bare stone walls. Max looked up the stairwell, trying to see how close Bruce was following them.

His shadow slid along the whitewashed cinder block, his stupid patchy beard appearing before his dumb face. "I'm sure you remember where they are. Keep moving until you can't anymore." He cinched his duffel bag higher on his shoulder as he spoke.

Max thought through the geometry. Bruce was walking opposite them, able to watch them as they descended. Each time the women reached a floor, Bruce arrived at the landing above. That's when she'd be out of his line of sight. That's when Max would act, while obscured from Bruce.

At another landing, Max lifted the tablet and opened the DOWN interface with a tap, springing the file explorer to the screen. Then she lowered the tablet, waiting to see if Bruce had noticed her actions.

"Why did they leave you?" Min called behind them. "And while we're at it, where did everyone go?"

"Why?" he hollered back. "Same reason they left your sorry asses here. They had to lay the blame on someone for the worst industrial accident in the history of humanity, didn't they? You, along with Waffel and Courgette, you created the portal technology that triggered the mishap with the Zero Point Module. They added me and my team to the leave-behind list because the ZPM was my design."

As if hearing him, the building rattled, sending the dog's tail between his legs as plumes of dust fell from the steps above Max's head.

After a hurried check that they were out of his view, Max drew the tablet. She entered two letters into the search bar before she reached the steps.

"Of course, that's bullshit. Everyone knows the ZPM safety protocols are perfection, but they had to put someone on the cross. Exile the sinners from Eden and whatnot," he continued.

Now he's Adam, himself! Passing another landing, she stole a glace up the spiraling gap, finding Bruce staring at the wall ahead of him.

"You couldn't convince them?" Min asked. It helped that she kept him pontificating and distracted.

"They didn't want to be convinced, you know? Made up their minds right when the ZPM breached. They needed someone to blame, to vindicate themselves."

The women circled another landing, Max entering the rest of her search before switch-backing to the next flight of steps. As soon as she was out of his sight line, she verified her typing in a rapid glance: OWNER:BRUCE GOSE.

"They took my plans with them, you know that, right? They blame me for Earth's demise. They leave me behind, but take my ZPM designs with them to power their new home. It's messed up and illogical."

Max agreed with him for once. It's easy to condemn the creator when an application of a technology goes awry. She touched the icon to execute the query, then muted the tablet's speaker in case the interface might chirp on a match.

"Especially considering it's *your* fault. The 'Four Whores of the Apocalypse'," he chided.

Max bit her tongue as any sympathy she felt for the misogynist burned away. Min cleared her throat, giving Max a firm gaze as she droned, "Yeah, we saw the poster in your workshop. So clever."

Next landing, Max checked the status of the search. Multiple hits, as she expected, sorted by date. The newest file was at the top: BOOM-VEST. *Subtle, Bruce.* She tapped the icon to open it, noting a message splashing the screen before she had to conceal the tablet once more.

Max processed the after image in a blink: DOWN was asking for a password.

Bruce continued to spew hate as Max reasoned what the file's password could be. Just this morning, Max had used his passcode for the fabricators to get around their materials quotas. It was the same password Bruce had given her when she had to fix his code for the assemblers last year. Reusing a password was the kind of arrogant behavior Max could rely on from Bruce!

But the events of the day had scrubbed her mind—*what the hell was that password?* She had one guess; the file lived on the tablet in Bruce's hand, and it would notify him if someone tried to access it without permission. *SomethingSomething69, wasn't it?*

The clop of her boots on the cement became a metronome, counting off the steps she had left to disable the explosive device. *What was it? ButtBandit69, something like that?*

"Just a couple more floors," he called. "When you hit the blockage, go through the door. Then down the hall about 30 meters."

CheekSeeker69? That was closer. The cadence felt right, at least.

"Then we'll all head to the Transfer Portal rooms, and you can watch me leave this shit-hole planet for someplace better. Somewhere people will respect me. Where I'll be up to my neck in tits and ass!"

Ass! AssMaster69! That was it! The memory clicked tight mere steps before the next landing, and it took every ounce of control Max had not to whip the tablet up and enter the password before they were out of his sight.

On the following landing, Max threw off all caution and tapped the password into the tablet. The file expanded, showing one line of meaningless characters and numbers. Rather than try to interpret the data, she opened the file's security parameters. She reset the password to a random mashing of her tablet's on-screen keyboard.

Whatever interface Bruce was using on the tablet, it could no longer edit the DOWN file. He had lost his ability to detonate the grenade.

"Holy shit!" The terror in Min's voice sucked Max out of her satisfaction. She looked up and gasped.

The stairs descended to a landing, identical to the dozens they'd passed on the way here. It was the far side that drew her attention. Blocking the steps beyond was a mass of woven branches. What looked to Max to be knotted brown knuckles. Were these the tendrils from outside? Had they pierced this building, too? Writhed up the stairwell to this floor?

Bork raced ahead, tail up and wagging in circles as he worked one of the thinner ones out of the knitted bramble. Max ran a tentative finger across the knobby skin of the closest tendril.

"It's... wood."

An odor rose, pungent and rich as coffee or spiced chocolate. Max couldn't place it.

"Barbecue," Min said. "It smells like a cookout."

That was it! Not the vaporous nastiness of lighter fluid, but the smoky and sweet fragrance of flavoring wood chips. "Why would the end of the world smell so delicious?"

"It's mesquite," Bruce hollered. "Every sample we've taken. It's all one giant mesquite tree. No idea where it came from. And it doesn't matter. Keep moving. Through the door and head right."

Max shelved the insane puzzle those wooden knots and fingers presented and snapped into the immediate problem. The command interface between the bomb and Bruce's tablet was inoperable. She took Min's shoulder, heaving her forward, almost causing her to tumble. Min shoved the door, and Max ushered her and the dog through.

The door slammed with an explosive report. "Go," she commanded over the echo. "The vest—Bruce can't trigger it anymore. Run!"

32

A Better Bad Idea

The corridor ended at a T-intersection. Min skidded to a stop, about to ask which direction they should go. Avoiding the debate, Max took her arm and steered her to the left. Behind them, the stairwell door crashed open.

"Get back here, bitches!" Bruce hollered down the hallway, his words loud and harsh and clear, even with the acoustic-dampening walls tamping his scream.

The corridor ahead did something Min had never seen on the Daft Institute campus: it curved. She had around fifty meters of visibility before the hallway's bend blocked her line of sight. There were no visible connecting corridors or doors.

"Where do we go?" she huffed. The grenade sat heavy and dangerous against her ribs, and running only slammed it harder into her body.

"Ahead is the only choice!"

A few meters in front of the women, Neils Bork padded to a halt. His nose probed the base of the wall on their right, and they saw what caught his interest.

A bay door. Immense and intimidating, and nothing like the lab entrances elsewhere in the building. It was at least twice her height, and with arms spread, she wouldn't be able to touch either end of it.

And there was no way to open the damned thing. No handle. No control pad.

"What is this?" she exclaimed. Her hands ran up the door's vertical seam, struggling to pry the two panels apart.

"Transfer Portal Sigma," Max read, her hand slapping the placard Min had missed. "Let's hope there's a Tau or a Rho, and that they're open!"

Max dragged her away from the door, deeper into the curving hallway. Another twenty meters and they found a second door—this one normal-sized and familiar. Min read the sign: STORAGE.

"We could hide in here," she offered.

Max was a few strides ahead, looking down the curve. "We're going to have to," she sighed. "Those weird branches are blocking the way."

Min closed the three steps to Max, revealing a mass of spindly wood a dozen meters away. It extended from floor to ceiling, occupying the entire width of the corridor.

Rapid, rhythmic thuds closed on them. Bruce was coming their direction.

"In here!" Min grasped the handle, heaved her shoulder into the door. Max and the dog bolted inside, and Min forced the door shut, stopping it from slamming and announcing their location.

Her fingers went for the lock, but found none. "We need something to block the door," she stressed.

A flatulent wail drew her gaze left, where Max crouched against the posts of an empty steel utility shelf. Her slight frame shoved into it, heaving with fits and starts towards the door. Each little shove caused the shelf to scrape the floor, emitting another tiny fart sound. "Little help?" she groaned.

Min grabbed the other set of risers and tugged. The shelf jerked closer.

"Hook the door handle," Max said. "It'll keep it from turning."

Min smiled at her friend's quick thinking. The shelf slid into place, with the riser slipping around the handle. Max reached in and gave the handle a test jiggle. It moved a few centimeters—not enough to unlatch the door. Bruce could still break his way through if he had more weapons in that satchel he was carrying, but this would have to do.

Min turned her attention to the bomb on her chest. Her fingers shot to the snap buckle at her waist, squeezing it until it clicked apart. Her frantic hands located another just under her shoulder. After she popped it, the entire vest slid off her frame and clattered to the floor.

Min collapsed next to the vest. For several uninterrupted seconds, she closed her eyes, inhaled and exhaled, her heart slowing to a reasonable rhythm, its thrush fading in her ears.

She couldn't dawdle; they were in endless danger from the approaching singularity and Bruce's bag of explosive tricks. She sucked in the calm, letting it seep from her chest into her limbs, which grew heavy and sank to the floor.

The peace ceased as a reverberation grew under her. Not an organic stress groan of the building, but mechanical and regular. She rolled to her side, ear on the tile, sensing the regular *chink-a-chink-a-chonk* of something mechanical.

"What is it?" Max asked.

"I think Bruce is opening that enormous door we passed," she replied. Min sat up, her gaze landing on the hydrobaric grenade in Max's demure hands. "What the hell are you doing with that?"

"Nothing yet, but I figured having our own explosive might even the odds with Bruce." Max gestured in a circle, presenting the vacant room to Min. "There's nothing else useful in here."

Min scanned the space for the first time. Several rows of bare shelves, same as the one securing the door. The only other stand-out features were the few spiraling wands of mesquite puncturing through the floor. Bork gnawed one knot with agitation as he watched the two women.

"We need to get into that room, Min. The aperture's in there."

Of course, she was right. If that room contained a working Foresight ring, it might be their only way home. "We don't know what other tricks Bruce has with him. He's a megalomaniacal asshat, but he isn't stupid. He'll have thought of contingencies."

Max patted the conical point of the device with her palm. "I think I understand how to use this. I mean, I'm assuming the obvious, here. Set this analog timer. Tick, tock. Then, *boom!*"

Min shifted her way onto her feet, an ache making her aware of every aching muscle and bone. Her eyes moved from the grenade to Max's needful stare. "I don't want to hurt anyone."

Max shrugged. "Me neither, but maybe the threat is enough to get what we need."

Min thought through the scenarios. "Sounds a bit 'wild west,' but I'm listening."

Max's gaze turned to the weapon. "Maybe we walk into the Transfer Portal Room with this thing set to blow in five seconds? Tell him to leave or I'll drop it?"

"Mutually assured destruction," Min sighed. Her mind raced, seeking to calculate probabilities without data. "Against an arrogant cowboy like Bruce, that feels like a bad, bad idea."

A wrinkle cracked across Max's brow. "You got a better bad idea?"

Min scanned the vapid space. Tallied their resources: empty shelves, two brilliant women, a good dog, a grenade capable of destroying water in an indeterminate radius, and a few serpentine branches poking through the crawlspace—one etched with Labrador teeth marks.

As she wracked her brain for a miracle, the rhythm of the mechanical song inverted. *Chonk-a-chonk-a-chink, chonk-a-chonk-a-chink.* The implication was clear: Bruce was closing the door to Transfer Portal Sigma.

As if Min needed more motivation, a second rumble came through the walls, rattling the metal shelves in their risers. Another seismic event.

"Bad-bad idea it is," she huffed. "Let's roll."

33

CALL INTO THE VOID

Bruce cursed as he stretched his arm deeper into the crawlspace. His fingers waggled, their tips probing for the round power connector that linked every device in the room to the building's main grid.

He knew *where* the connector was. The problem was getting access to it among all the damned branches and roots that had sprouted through the floors. He spat again, wishing he had brought some physical hand tools with him—a set of metal snips would have been ideal, or even wire cutters. Hell, hacking at the growth with his vintage soldering iron would be better than this!

His middle finger hooked the curved lip of the connector, the hard flange leading to the round, flat surface. He was close. Needed just another centimeter of reach to pinch the safety tabs and rotate the connector 90 degrees to release it. He pressed his shoulder into the bramble, his other hand gripping a thick limb to get some leverage. Behind him, the bay doors for the Transfer Portal room were crawling shut.

The knotty wood and toothy bark scraped his neck and arm until his fingers pinched the connector's edge. A squeeze—a twist—and the thing was free!

He eased the cable towards him, feeling the slack ebb and flow as it threaded through the rough branches. His arm wrenched out of the burrow, skin grated and pink. The power connector emerged, and he let go of his held breath.

He lurched up, and his free hand shot into his duffel. He rooted until he found the smooth metal of a ZPM bottle.

A noise echoed from the hallway—a clatter and bang that told him the women were coming. He needed to get energy flowing. Trigger the emergency door release and isolate himself.

The bottle snapped onto the connector, and the room blanched with white light. The whispering hum of the air processors blanketed the inert silence.

Bruce scrambled to his feet. Stumbling across the precarious floor, broken and unsteady from the undergrowth, his gaze locked on the big red plunger button beside the massive bay doors.

Colors shifted in his periphery, but he stayed focused. Three strides away.

Shadows in the hallway. Dark forms taking shape. Expanding and closing. Two strides now.

Shouting. Noise from the women. One last leap.

His fist launched. Connected with the plunger. Over the battle cries of Min and Max erupted a harrowing squeal as the emergency door pneumatics engaged. Bruce turned to catch the pleading eyes of Minerva. The door snapped closed less than a meter in front of her face.

• • • ● ●• ● ● • ••

"No!" Min cried. "Dammit!" Her palms *whomped* against the door, the sound muffled and demure given her rage.

"Min?" Max cried.

Min screamed into the door. Max flinched at her rage. Even Bork took a few clumsy pads away, ears pinned to his skull.

Max pleaded with her again, stepping back until she found the wall.

But Min wasn't listening. Her hands slapped the seam. Fingers dug into the unyielding polymer. Arms strained to tear the doors apart.

"Min!" she wailed, sliding down the wall until she hit the floor.

The physicist finally spun. Her eyes saucered, brow knitted with disbelief. "What are you doing? Help me, Max!"

Max shook as her vision blurred. She held up her hands. One holding the grenade's primary grip; the other clamped around the other end. "I can't," she sobbed. "I set the timer on this. As soon as I let go, it'll activate!"

• • • ●•●● • ••

Min felt the color seep from her face.

"I'm sorry," Max pleaded. "I thought we were going to make it!"

"How long?"

Max slid her gaze to the tip of the conical weapon, slipped a finger up to read the timer. Her eyelids clamped shut and her head tapped the wall. "Five seconds."

Shit. Min's thoughts cycled into overdrive. "Can you cancel it? Extend it?"

"If it's possible, I don't know how. Min I'm sorry!"

Shit! The door punched her lumbar as Min landed against it. "We won't outrun that blast in five seconds," she thought aloud.

Max nodded as a tear seeped from her eye. "We didn't think this through."

She was right. They were desperate, and had made desperate choices. And now their situation was deteriorating.

"Hello, bitches!" Bruce's voice boomed from the door at her back. Min flinched, then crab-crawled over to Max against the opposite wall.

"What the shit?" she gasped.

"I didn't realize these bay doors had surface transducers built into them," he continued. "I'm glad they do, though. It lets me chat with you while I secure my future."

"Shut the fuck up!" Min screamed.

"Oh, hey! I can hear you too!" Bruce laughed. "That makes this even more fun!"

Min cursed. She needed clarity. Not Bruce Goose taking a dump on her thoughts.

"I know we can't see each other. This will have to do for our last goodbyes." His playful voice was a twisting knife.

Before Min could curse a response, he continued, "So I've got the room powered, right? And I'm feeding one of the Transfer Portal initiation routines I scraped off of Waffel's office computer into the control terminal."

A buzz rocked the doors; Min realized it was Bruce chuckling.

"I can't say I understand how these portals work, but based on her notes and procedures, I don't think Waffel did, either. Fucking typical of you lot. Isn't it?"

Max sobbed next to her. Min looked over to see her arms shaking as her tight clutch held the grenade firm.

"Always taking credit for things you didn't do, or applying solutions you don't comprehend." His tone remained matter-of-fact. Min imagined he was running through an aperture startup checklist like they used in the Foresight lab. "Never giving respect to the giants on whose shoulders you stand."

A vibration came through the floor. Steady and pure, Min recognized it: the aperture powering up.

"Ah, there we go." Bruce's distracted voice echoed from the doors. "As I was saying, it's *my* zero-point power source that made your technology useful. My *mind* that gave you any sort of purpose. And you abused it, dooming us all."

Min scrambled to her feet. Paced the length of the door, as if building momentum to plow through it. Bork padded out of her path, monitoring her movement.

"You two deserve to die. Several times, if that were possible. Starve in this wasteland. Then get cooked by X-rays from the singularity. Reborn to be crushed in a gravity press. Shoot, I'd give my nuts to have you both live for an eternity, floating in the empty aftermath of what you've created here!"

Min stopped. Rested her head against the door seam, palms on either side, rage bubbling up her throat. The frequency of the aperture's vibrations rose. Bruce was increasing the power to the ring.

"On second thought, I'll keep my balls. I plan to use them a lot. Wherever this claptrap takes me, I'm going to be smothered in pussy!"

The bubbles in her gut exploded. Min banged her fists against the door and screamed, "I hope you drown in it!"

• • • ● • ● • • •

The reverberation shook the room, surpassing the growing rattle of the portal's hum. Her outburst had tickled him. He relished he would be the last human contact they would have. That they'd die knowing he was smarter than they were. More successful. Their final thoughts spent wishing they *were* him.

He set the final power level progression for the portal, double-checking against the procedure copied from Waffel's computer. Then he turned to the door, cupped his hands around his mouth, and hollered, "Just so you know, I would have fucked either of you. All you had to do was ask."

The ring's hum rose in pitch as his smiling maw returned to the control panel. Power levels were steady, and the twelve-foot portal set before the far wall was displaying some spatial aberrations. Gleams of light traced away from its middle, more and more of them appearing as the ring did whatever it does.

I hope you drown in it. Min's words made another pass through his mind, and his smile broadened. Drowning in pussy sounded like a fine way to die. One he would get behind. *Pun intended.*

In a blink, the radiating halo cleared, leaving a dark void filling the chrome circle.

His smile fell, and his certainty faltered. What was this? He expected to see... something. Anything. A room or airlock. At least a person. Any concrete object would be more welcome than the null space before him.

His thoughts shifted back to the catastrophe, months ago. The OTO turning black as pitch, then belching death across the planet. His eyes narrowed and searched for movement.

"Hello?" he called out. He rounded the control terminal, stepping to the portal for a better view of the emptiness inside. He waited for a response or an echo over the thrum of energy cycling around the ring.

Nothing came. Then a flicker—fingers of refracted light deep in that dark, revealing hints of rich blues and greens beyond. Bruce eased closer, trying to glimpse some detail inside of that dimness.

The hum stopped. The visage inside of the ring appeared to stiffen. And then the room exploded around him.

34

Bruce's Win

The door screamed. Bruce's scream, cut short by a percussive and thick *slap* on the other side of the door. A crippling silence followed.

Min backed away, confused. Behind her, she sensed Max scrambling upright.

The doors groaned. Not the surface transducer conveying sound from the room inside—this was the rising tension of stress, a crescendo of imminent destruction.

A chill wrapped over her feet. Min stared down. Her sneakers disappeared into a growing puddle of foam bubbling up through the floor.

Something freezing sprayed her face. She raised a palm to block it, tracing it to the seam between the doors.

The bay doors that were bulging outward. The spew expanding as the doors split apart.

Min spun, grabbed Max by the wrist. Pivoted to see Bork bolting down the corridor. Leading them away from what was about to happen.

She pumped her legs. Two strides in and a volcano of noise erupted. The squeal of shearing metal, the throaty crack of tearing plastics, and a belching roar she registered before a wall of fury heaved her forward.

Her balance shifted, orientation inverted. The floor rushed up, and Min clenched her eyes for the impact. Instead of a punch in the face, a chill slapped every millimeter of skin. A deafening scream surrounded her, swallowing her up. The clamor and cold compressed her as she spiraled through the air.

Not air, she realized. Too heavy. Too thick.

Water. Icy, bone-pricking, sense-shocking water surrounded her. Swatted her down the corridor. Knees and chin to her chest, she tucked into a tight ball before the rushing force slammed her against a wall.

· · · ● · ● · · ·

The grenade she'd held in a desperate death grip slipped away in a froth of fury and motion that lifted Max off the floor and spun her around.

The air in the corridor solidified. Vision blurred and sound closed in as the hallway burst full of water.

Freezing needles pierced every patch of her skin, shoved her to the floor, and she gasped.

Her lungs screamed, and Max knew she had made a mistake. She flew along the corridor, moving at the whim of the current barreling into her, and she realized she was drowning.

Her eyes scoured the spinning hallway for some sign of Bork. Or Min. Directions were meaningless as she tumbled end over end. Her mind registered the fan of Bork's bean-shaped toe pads passing in front of her as the shock of the freezing water tricked her into inhaling another lungful.

A weight slammed her down, a rush of water shoved her into the floor. Under the panic, the inability to think, a calm took root in her chest.

This is how I die. The thought arrived without judgment or fear; it was just a fact. One of several as a brilliant green glow surrounded her:

I love you, Bork. I love you, Min. Sorry for all the fuss today. It's kind of my fault.

As she accepted her fate, a fresh fear bubbled. Between the timid facts in her head, Max recognized the lime-stained light slicing through the water. The same putrid shade that had covered the walls of the Foresight control room.

It was the exploding hydrobaric grenade.

· · ● ● · ● ● · · ·

The violence thrashing her body shifted, yanking Min back instead of pressing her against the wall. Still helpless, Min waited for the final blow. Hoped for unconsciousness before she inhaled water and drowned.

Instead, the crushing cold released. The immense pressure dissipated, replaced by a sudden tropical warmth that left her floating. Not in water, but through the air once more.

Still curled up, confused by the rapid change in sensation, she took the impact on her spine. A shredding abrasion raked her shoulders as she skidded along the floor.

She unrolled as she landed, arms expanding, body slapping prone. All the random forces on her were gone, the roar in her ears replaced by a burning sting over her torso. She lay there, unsure for how long. Seconds? Minutes?

An abrasive grit stung the heels of her hands. She tried opening her eyes, but they resisted as if glue covered her eyelashes. Her fingertips rubbed at it, and a solid mass crumbled away, allowing her eyes to peel open.

Her gaze floated to her pain: palms raw with road rash, abraded with hundreds of thin and painful gouges. The skin on her back burned with fresh scrapes, too. A white sand disintegrated off of her as she lifted her arm.

Snow? It was too warm, the air too sticky and thick.

She tasted it now as she breathed: salt. Briney and metallic on her palette. She sat up. A flaccid green light illuminated the hallway. Except it wasn't a hallway anymore. It was a cave. The rectangular frame and subtle curve Min recognized under the caked coating of small white crystals covering every surface. Through the curve, a glare sparkled off of the countless small facets coating the walls. Even the air glowed, wisps of light bending around her as particulate steams ebbed and flowed.

A frantic scratching rose. Then the high-tension whine of a dog in distress echoed from beyond the curve.

"Bork," she coughed into the thick air. "I hear you." Min wobbled upright on the uneven floor. She stepped forward, layers of blanched soot cracking off of her clothing as the piles of salts shifted under her sneakers.

After a dozen stumbling meters, she found the dog. His fur wasn't yellow anymore, but caked in greenish-white. Bork scoured into a drift of salt against the outside wall, his paws scattering powder behind him. As Min got close, she understood the dog's panic.

From under the mound of pale and earthy powder, flesh protruded. Max's tiny and still hand.

· • • ● ● ● ● • • ·

Seconds later, Max's head was visible. She laid face-down, entombed. Min tore the foreign matter away until her arm could wrap the woman's delicate waist.

She heaved. The briny sand held the engineer tight. Min repositioned herself, straddling Max's encased body to use her powerful legs, and she heaved once more. The salt crumbled away, and Max came free.

Min examined the rag doll in her arms. Max wasn't conscious. A close look at her face, brushing away the crystals stuck there, Min realized her friend wasn't breathing.

Min cried out, a desperate sound. She rolled Max over, getting her on a flat stretch of ground. Her fingers shot to Max's neck. A few seconds of waiting, and Min found what she sought.

A pulse!

Her hand shot under Max's neck, tilting the woman's chin up to open her airway before clamping her nostrils closed. Min sucked in a tangy lungful of air, then wrapped her mouth over Max's. She heaved out the breath against immense resistance as her friend's chest expanded from the force.

Max's body jolted, and Min broke away. Water sprayed out of the engineer's mouth, a trickle at first. Min helped the woman onto her side, and a steady flow of liquid sputtered out of Max as she wracked with coughs.

She eased off, keeping her hands ready to prevent Max from rotating back. It was all up to her now. She needed to expel whatever it was in her lungs. After an eternity of struggling, the engineer steadied into a tentative cadence of phlegmy breaths.

Min's muscles loosened. The wave of relief cascaded over her. She collapsed against the drift, ignoring the pinch of pain as her raw back touched the salt. She breathed, mimicking the shallow pattern of Max's hitched inhales and wet exhales. Then, Max eased herself seated next to Min. Bork approached, scouring Max's cheek and hair with his searching nose.

The engineer took it in: the white crumbs on her clothes, in her hair, the particulates on her skin. Her tongue probed her lips as Bork cleaned her face.

"Salt?" she coughed.

"I don't understand it, either," Min said. Her breath grated her throat.

"I think I do," Max sputtered. "The grenade... slipped out of my hands when you pulled on me." She turned away from Transfer Portal Room Sigma's battered doors, lifting a wobbling hand toward the puke-green glow down the corridor. "The torrent rushed it that way."

Min's brain clicked it together. "Salt water? When the grenade ignited, it consumed the water, leaving this precipitate behind?"

Max nodded, head turning back and resting on the drift behind them. Her fingers moved to Bork's furry neck, pulling the dog close.

"And the water came from..." Min voiced the question for which she knew the answer.

"Where else?" Max's tone fell as she called Min out. "Where else would it have come from?"

The aperture. The goddamned aperture unleashed another torrent of destruction.

"I don't think we grok how those rings work," Max croaked.

Min snorted, her nose dry and sinuses chapped. "I'd say we've verified that hypothesis. Multiple times over."

"One thing I know for certain?" Max continued as she ran her fingers through Bork's fur. A powdery salt grime rose out of his fur with each stroke. "That's the only time that Bruce Goose has gotten a woman wet."

35

BITE THE DUST

"It's still in one piece," Min called. Max raised her head, seeing Min picking at the close edge of the aperture in Transfer Portal Room Sigma. "Can it work with the coils encased in salt? Is the salt more conductive than the vanadium dioxide?"

Max rose and dusted off her cargo pants. "Doesn't matter," she replied. "The main coupling is destroyed. If the floor wasn't full of branches, and salt, and random slabs of what I'm assuming is fish jerky, I could find a different way to get one of our power bottles wired into the ring. As it is, though, I'd need to go upstairs to fetch some tools."

Min nodded. "Well, this is room Sigma. Think there's a Rho? Or a Tau?"

Max tried to ignore dust and kipple in the trashed room. She examined the shape and geometry of the space and found a wide slice of pie: the bay doors built into the outer crust, and an enormous aperture at the fruity tip. "This room is about a fourth of a circle, isn't it? And yeah, the corridor keeps going around in both directions."

Min approached, gesturing at the blown-out doors. "Think they're locked, too?"

Max spat the excessive salty tang off her tongue. "Bruce seemed to believe so. Let's locate another Transfer Portal Room, then see what's what."

• • • ● • ● • ● • •

The ominous green haze created by the hydrobaric weapon had dissipated. Min slipped her tablet out and powered the work light. In the razing white of the tablet's LED, the crystalline facets of the salt sparkled. If she hadn't been exhausted, and if the seismic tremors hadn't been increasing in frequency and magnitude, Max would have found the place kind of magical.

"It's pretty," she murmured.

Min turned to her. "It's what, now?"

Max shrugged. "I mean, with the light, this is amazing-looking, isn't it? Like a fantasy world. I expect to run into a unicorn around the next corner."

Min hacked out a wad of phlegm. When she spoke, her voice rattled. "A unicorn would not surprise me. Not after today. The shock would be if the unicorn *didn't* want to kill us."

The salt walls had been closing in as they moved further down the hall. Max estimated the space was about half its original width. The women could still walk side-by-side, but Bork trotted ahead of them.

"Look," Min said, pointing at a streak of dirty gray, stark along the powdery pale floor. "Wood dust. Remember the branches blocking the hallway?"

Max looked around the walls and ceiling. More signs of the strange wood clung above them: countless shriveled little fingers and knots gripping into the salt over their heads. Against the briny odor of the air, her nose picked up a fruity and rich vapor. "The grenade must have ended up near here when it detonated," she remarked.

Both women froze as a peculiar clatter came from the tunnel ahead.

"Oh fuck, is that Bruce? Did he survive?"

"*We* survived it," Min said, crouching as if she could hide her filthy clothes and bloody skin against the white canvas around her.

The tension dissolved as Bork's playful *boof* echoed in front of them.

Max chuckled with relief. "It's only Neils Bork."

They paced ahead; the light revealed a sharp expansion of the salt. Min held out a hand, stopping Max from walking over a drop-off two strides away.

About a meter below them, Bork pranced across the Daft Institute's standard floor, the clatter of his nails on a solid surface novel after the shush of the sandy grains under their feet. Clamped in his jaw was a length of mesquite branch, and in his eyes was the pride of a dog rewarded.

"You found a stick," Max cooed, the edema in her chest making it sound gruff and watery. "Because you're a good boy!"

Bork released the stick and approached. His attention had left the women, and focused on the plateau of salt upon which they stood. Max looked down. Her dog studied the edge of the mound with tentative sniffs.

"Shine the light there," she directed with her finger. The LED washed over the sandy slope, shifting from the pale white to a muddy brown at the base of the drop-off. A royal blue sneaker lay on the floor.

"Bruce," Min gasped. Her palm went to her mouth in shock.

Max nodded. *Good riddance.*

The dog's snout moved to another off-color patch, just outside the light. Min followed with the LED. "Oh, boy."

An empty pant leg lay exposed from the salt pile, lined up with the shoe as if Bruce's chicken leg was still there.

Max squatted on her haunches and slid to the bottom of the slope. She landed next to the crime scene, easing Bork back a step so she could investigate.

"I don't see a body," she reported. She tapped the shoe with her boot, then toed the fabric of the leg. Both flopped loose and empty.

"Uh, I'm pretty sure it's there," Min called down. "This close to the blast, it probably dehydrated him into dust."

Max squinted, lowering closer to the clothing without blocking the light. "He'd been carrying the passkey on a carabiner, hooked to his belt loop. I can't see it, but..." She stood, her hand plucking up the free pant leg and giving it a test yank.

The salt pile gave up a few inches of fabric, so she heaved. A cloud of gray dust billowed from the trousers. Max dropped the pants. Her hands shot over her face, eyes clamped shut as her brain registered that the tang in the airborne haze was the remains of Bruce.

She gagged. Atoms of the man floated in her sinuses. In her lungs. She stumbled, her leg tapping Bork as she lost her bearings.

A grip took her. The familiar cradle of Min's support leading her away from the cloud. "This way. Just a few steps."

The wall was at her back, Min easing her to the floor as her fingers wiped the rancid particulates off of her face. Shaking the matter from her hair. Wiping her eyes with her shirt.

"Wait here," Min said. "I'll check for the passkey."

Max's stomach churned, threatening to heave. She creaked open her eyes to ground herself, discovering Bork sitting across from her, looking concerned. When their gaze met, the dog's tail beat the floor. Max usually found the rhythm calming. With her roiling stomach, the cadence irritated her.

Min's grunt pulled her attention. With her shirt collar hiked over her mouth and nose, she had the pants free, pulled from the rubble by the heel of her sneaker. She nudged them away from the settling particles.

The vibrations from Bork's tapping rattled Max's gut. "Please stop, Bork."

Min's tight lips erupted in a grin. "Jackpot!" she said, as she bent down to the waist of the empty pants. When she spun around, the passkey dangled from the carabiner looped on her finger.

Bork's rattle expanded. Max turned, ready to scold the dog, only to find him backing away, ears pinned and eyes on a wide swivel, scouring the area for danger.

Vibrations carried into the air, and Max realized a steady stream of salt was falling from the ceiling above them. "Oh shit," she huffed, struggling to her unsteady feet. "More seismic waves!"

Min was already jogging past. "We need to find another aperture, now!"

36

Happy Thoughts

"There's Tau!" Min shouted over the steady rumble. She lifted the passkey, gaze bouncing from the rectangular dongle to the smooth bay doors as she realized the problem. "What the hell do I do with this thing?" She tapped it against the massive door. Held it firm against the polymer surface for a pregnant second. "How does it open?"

Max leapt ahead to the seam where the two doors met and spread her fingers. After a moment of searching, she found a small indentation several centimeters long. "Here," she suggested, her finger stuck about chest-high.

Min pressed the flat key to the spot, and the snap of a magnet yanked it from her grasp. Something squealed in the door, followed by the cyclic churn of a motor engaging.

The seam parted, and Min felt relief, and then panic again. The doors were opening. Really. Fucking. Slowly.

Dust cascaded over them, the building unable to stop for breath as the ground undulated beneath it. An image of the three of them trapped in a shaking snow globe passed through Min's head as she waited... and waited for the door to allow them to pass.

Through that narrow opening, the tablet's LED showed clean lines of floor tiles unscathed by wood or water or salt. An aperture, tall and wide enough to drive a bus through, glinted in response to her light.

"Room looks intact." She had to shout her words over the growing ambient grind. "As soon as you can get through, wire up a bottle. I'll prep the startup sequence on my tablet."

Max nodded, fingers moving to the bulging pocket on her pants leg as if reminding herself the power bottles were there. She twisted sideways and squeezed through the narrow gap between the opening bay doors. A heavy crash further down the hallway drew Min's attention: a slab of ceiling had broken loose, fallen the five meters to the floor. When she turned back, Bork's tail was slipping through the doors as well.

She needed more space before her larger frame would fit. Min pulled her tablet from her pocket, thankful the BigWheels controller contained military-grade electronics and hardware able to withstand the trials of the day. She loaded up the data from their aperture start-up routine.

Min coded the power-up sequence, finishing just as light poured through the opening bay doors. As if realizing the surrounding danger, they slid open in a matter of seconds. She raced into Transfer Portal Room Tau. Her gaze shot across the space, finding Max rising to her feet.

"Juice is on," she called. Her finger pointed at a podium a few feet from her. "That must be the control console."

Min moved to the console, already cycling through its boot-up routine. Two shaking breaths later, she had a terminal open and was scouring the list of commands and files for something familiar.

Max stumbled next to her as Min wiped the crumbles and dust off the screen. "The tremors are getting worse!"

"I think I've got it," Min hollered over the blooming rumble. The command and file structure appeared close to the protocols they used in the Foresight lab. She accessed the start-up program on her tablet using the DOWN, made a few necessary tweaks, and gave it one last look.

"Are you sure this will work?" Max cried. Her hand gripped the edge of the podium to brace against the building's constant movement. "This will get us home?"

"It's our best guess, Max. We're doing exactly what got us here."

Max's eyes piqued as her cheeks rattled with the quake. "Happy thoughts?" she shrugged.

Min took in her friend. Vivacious and somehow demure on a regular day, now Max was in tatters. Skin caked and chapped. Body bruised. She had drowned and been entombed in salt. And yet here she was, her smirk opening the split in her lips, bringing hope to this miserable situation.

"Happy thoughts," Min confirmed. She executed the aperture startup program.

Min wasn't sure it was working. She strained to hear the hum of the ring sucking up power over the expanding quake, see any aberration inside of the aperture over the constant crumbling structure.

A blink later, the first shimmers appeared. Rippling halos followed.

"It's working," she cried. She rounded the console to get a better view, and the rising hum of the powering aperture joined the tremors rattling her bones. Max bolted ahead of her, gathering Bork by the scruff of his neck and hugging him close. "A few more seconds!"

Happy thoughts. Min's mind sought them out: the thrill of discovery; a warmth from collaborating with helpful and kind people; the joy of knowing they were making the world a better place.

The positive thoughts stalled when the floor heaved beneath her. Min fell prone against the tile as it shifted like liquid. New shadows danced around her, and Min's gaze rose to catch the iridescent waves of light calming into a solid surface within the ring.

The light disappeared. Min stood, frozen with fear. In place of the blue-white glow, there was a barren emptiness. No clean room. No polymer paneling. No ramp to guide the rover through the ring. Only a bottomless unknown. Like the OTO before it unleashed hell on Earth.

Min's heart clenched. Rubble cascaded around her as the quake intensified. "What do we do?" she screamed. She turned, searching for Max.

Amid the dropping dust and concrete, Max cowered over her dog, shielding the animal from the loose bits of the building coming apart.

Through the rabble came a new sound. A second growing roar that pressed down from above. The crescendo of destruction was closing on them from all directions.

"The building is coming down!" Her scream was a drop in an ocean of cacophony. Min struggled against the shaking ground to reach her friends. One hand clutched Bork's scruff, the other Max's collar.

She heaved them away from the promise of oblivion, toward the unknown beyond the aperture. Three strides in, Min closed her eyes as they hit a curtain of falling chaff. Something shoved hard against her, forcing her to suck in a lung full of acrid dust.

Her feet failed her. Her hands slipped from her friends. The floor punched her, and a realization pierced her mind: *we are done-for.*

The screech of death erupted everywhere. A vigorous wind warned of imminent destruction. Her hands covered her head. Wave after wave of debris grated her exposed skin. The agony of the crumbling planet reached unbearable volumes.

And then it was over. All at once came a quiet. A stillness. She held her breath, mind floating in nothing.

I'm dead. This is death. Silent, dark. Forever. The thoughts circled in a low orbit, drowning bugs heading for the drain, until her screaming lungs forced her to gasp.

Her eyes stuttered open, hands finding the floor. It was pitch black, and she had no sense of the surrounding space.

Her ears detected a hum flitting atop the silence. One she would have taken for granted any other day: the subdued purr of Daft Institute air recyclers.

Light eased from above, and Min could see falling particulates racing away. As the illumination expanded, she could track dust disappearing into the vents between polymer wall panels.

The layout of the room was familiar. This was Transfer Portal Room Tau—the same footprint, but clean and empty. A few spots of small rubble, but no branches or salt. Min turned, sitting on her haunches. There was no window hanging in the air behind them. And no physical aperture framing it.

But there was someone. Max, prone on the floor. And sprawled beside her, Bork. Min stared, focusing on their chests, monitoring for the slightest motion to show that they were alive.

The LEDs continued to bloom. Along with the light came sounds. Hydraulic squelches. Snips and squeaks like Max's boots on the control room floor. Min pivoted to find figures approaching out of the gloom.

"Stay where you are," called a stranger's voice. More light filled the space, and the people solidified. Five of them. Battle fatigues. Tactical vests similar to the one Bruce forced on her. And each carried an assault weapon, their gaping barrels aimed at Min's face.

She raised her shaking hands to shield against the light and bullets.

"Do not move," the woman boomed. "I *will* shoot you!"

The command wracked through Min, lashing at her ears. The more she tried to calm herself, the more her bones shook in her skin.

"Easy, Sergeant," crooned another woman, silhouetted in back-light. "I doubt they pose a threat. They appear injured." The shadow turned. "Officer Gelding? Please get in here."

That voice. Like so much of this room, Min recognized it. Not the same voice Min had heard days earlier. Or had it been years at this point? Her darkening gaze probed the liminal gray space, seeking the source. The shadow approached, passing the closest soldier. Min forced her failing eyes to focus.

Her lip trembled as a smile eased into her cheeks. "Oh, thank God," she whispered before collapsing at Dr. Waffel's feet.

37

Solve для E

"Six years."

Waffel's words stung in the only place Min wasn't sore: her hope.

"Come again?" Max asked.

"We discovered the rift six years ago," Waffel repeated. "Could have been there longer. It was hovering in a corner of an unused storage area. We only noticed it after testing a new Hawking sensor design in an adjacent room, trying to get clean baseline data."

"We had the portal powered for... what do you think, Max? Two minutes?"

"If that," Max confirmed, flinching from the antiseptic-laced cotton ball the medic was applying to the cracked skin on her chin.

Waffel nodded. Her eyes were striking and soft and framed with crow's feet. "Once we identified it, we reconfigured the room for containment and study. We've got more instrumentation on the rift you opened than on any other anomaly in history. We detected radiation coming through immediately. Particulates started arriving a few months later."

Min took another long pull from her water bottle, the added hydration accelerant leaving a piney tang on her tongue as she swallowed. "Was there a pattern to it?"

"The frequency and volume of matter emitted from the anomaly grew at a predictable rate. The AI ran countless models on the data, and they all pointed to the same thing. We knew *something* was happening today. We never had a handle on what, though. None of us expected the two of you."

"Three," Max corrected. Min glanced over to see Max's bare toes caressing the dog's chest. Bork's injuries had needed suturing, too. Patched up, he snoozed in front of Max's medical chair.

"Indeed." Waffel's smile carried genuine warmth and concern.

Min wondered how much their disappearance had affected the woman. Had the incident softened her edge? Or was this a natural shift that came with age?

"What happened in the Foresight lab?" Min asked. "That aperture must have been active for years, too."

"Five years," Max added. "According to our instrumentation."

"Did you keep it powered, hoping we'd come back?" Min followed.

More lines appeared across Shauna's brow. "We can talk about it all later. There's plenty we want to figure out. But the priority is your well-being. We're letting you rest here in Medical while Officer Gelding tends to your bodies. When she gives the okay, we'll set you up in a staff suite."

Her warm smile faltered. "And I'm required to tell you we will monitor your movements, as well as your body telemetry. For security. I'm sorry, but Daft has specific procedures in place around this anomalous event. For your safety and ours, we must proceed with caution."

Min swallowed her chuckle. The Shauna Waffel she spoke to days ago was crass, self-important, indignant, and proud. This woman had lived twelve years believing she'd driven the two women into a huge mistake. She had become empathic and kind, and many other things Min never associated with her advisor.

Waffel's hands found her lab coat pockets. "I'm calling in the big guns to help figure this out. It'll take a few days to round them up.

Until then, rest. And maybe answer a few questions when you're up to it."

Min adjusted the twist out of the medical gown, removing the cinch from her waist as she stood. "Thank you, Dr. Waffel. We could use some sleep, I think."

"And food," Max concurred. "For puppies, too," she cooed to Bork's twitchy dreaming body.

"Yes, of course," Dr. Waffel said. She lighted from the tall stool, her heels tapping the floor as she prepared to take her leave. "And you don't have to call me doctor. Everyone calls me Eta."

Min's brow wrinkled, releasing another sting as the antiseptic gel kissed her abraded skin. "Why would I call you Eta? Not Shauna?"

She stopped on her way out of Medical, turned, and smirked. "Shauna's my middle name. Eta's my first."

Max leaned forward, teetering on the edge of her chair. "Your name is *Eta Waffel?*"

It had been an ongoing mystery for as long as Min had known her advisor. *What does the 'E' stand for?* Dr. Waffel rarely added it to her signature, saving it only for legal and official government documentation, and even there, she only used the abbreviated letter. E. SHAUNA WAFFEL. And now Min saw why. The phonetics made her name sound like "ate a waffle."

It was a stupid thing that no one should care about. It's a name, that's all. But Waffel had rules for herself on these kinds of things. *Don't give people any reason to demean you; if they want to tread that path, force them to create their own.* Min tried to fathom the depth of change in the woman to account for the reversal of a core tenant. What would have to happen to Min to evoke such a transformation?

Waffel's gaze jumped to the Medical Officer. "Send me their instrumentation and bio-stats as soon as you have it, Gelding."

Then again, some things never change.

38

∆STRON∆UTS ∆ND ∆STRONOM∈RS

"I've never heard of a staff suite, much less seen one." Max's fingertips explored the solid wood dresser, then her eyes wandered to the plush bedding. The room was industrial, but well-appointed. Two queen beds, each with real cotton sheets and adaptive weighted blankets. A full shower and bath. Dual terminals with isolated acoustics. "This place is nicer than my apartment."

"Same," Min mumbled from the bathroom. Brushing her teeth was the first thing Min did after settling into the room. Max had an itch to scour off every particle of the future from her skin. One long run under a scalding shower to burn it away. But this was Min's third round of brushing.

We're doing the best we can, she reminded herself.

Max spun and fell onto a bed. Without asking for permission, Neils Bork followed her, nestling into her body and providing warmth and comfort.

She grabbed the remote keyboard from her bedside and powered on the large terminal mounted on the wall at the foot of her bed. Three seconds into the boot sequence, an error message appeared, telling her that the terminal had no network or local file access.

Damn. She wanted information. A date. Some scrap of news. Anything to fill in the missing years. *So wait, does that mean I'm still 26, or am I for-realsies at least 32 now? Is that how the time stuff works out?*

She caught a sense of why Min avoided temporal physics. Even the simplest question turned loaded.

Min appeared around the corner, spreading another layer of Gelding's cream on the rashy skin of her arms. She watched Max replace the keyboard on her nightstand. "No access?"

Max raked her frustrated fingers through her hair. "It was a long shot. I'd love a bit of data to process."

"I was hoping for the same." Min sat on her bed, across from Max.

Max eased to sitting, forcing Bork to shift. She mimicked Min's posture: feet grounded, hands clutching the mattress as if the bed were going to buck her off. The women locked eyes, and Max recognized the weariness on her friend. She was bone-tired, too.

And under that fatigue lurked something darker and thicker. Demanding to be acknowledged despite her exhaustion.

Guilt.

"I'm really sorry," she murmured. "It's my fault we're here."

Min shook her head. "We both got ourselves into this-"

Max held up a palm. "No, this is on *me*. I'm the one who kept pushing it. I hacked the fabricators to build the ring that caused this. I stole the bottle from Bruce. This is all my fault, Min."

Min's lip narrowed as she pulled at it with her teeth. A tell that she wanted to speak, but Max had to get this splinter out of her mind.

"Because I wanted my dead dog back. Or a clone of him, I suppose. Hell, if I had known Daft was continuing its cloning programs, I would have donated Bork's remains. Turned him into my little doggie Jango Fett."

Bork's paw pressed into Max's lumbar—the dog reacting to hearing his name.

"I'm so stupid, Min. I risked everything. We survived, but I ruined our lives."

Silence passed, expanding the cleft of remorse in her chest.

After several breaths, Min cleared her voice. She had something to say. "Do you know what you are, Max?"

Max knitted her brows. "I'm not sure what you-"

"You're an astronaut. An amazing, rocket-riding, shooting-star-chasing astronaut. Going to planets. Smelling the cosmos. Feeling the universe. Adapting to it. You've got to touch something before you believe it. Experience it for yourself to make it real."

Max swallowed, uncertain how to take Min's words.

"I'm not an astronaut," she continued. "Minerva Draper is certified to be 100% astronomer. I *observe* the universe. Measure frequencies or lumens or angular momentum or star wobble. Abstract all of it until we can fit it in our heads, and then build amazing things with that knowledge to improve people's lives."

Max studied her for an emotional tell. A curve of cheek, a narrowing of eyes. Min remained inscrutable, her gaze held on Max.

"I'm not saying either is better. I don't think that at all. If anything, they need each other."

Intrigue tugged on Max, and the gorge of her guilt narrowed. "Go on."

"It's a natural balance of observation and experience. Each feeds the other. The astronomer grounds the astronaut. No pun intended. And the astronaut gives the astronomer hope."

"Hope?"

"Of course. What's the point of finding a planet, a star, a galaxy, or a strange extra dimension, unless we have people who want to touch it? Go to it. Or exploit it."

"But we can't do those things."

"Not yet. But you can bet your ass that someone's working on it. Astronomers are working on it. Because somewhere, there's an astronaut who *wants* it to be possible."

A small bloom of joy opened in Max's chest. Min had never shared this philosophy. She never made Max feel inferior, inside or outside the lab; instead, Max did that to herself. Min was smarter than Max, at least in academics. Taller, and prettier by most standards. Educated, instead of fly-by-night learn-as-you-go. And Max knew she could learn from Min's kindness and patience.

But Min had never declared their equality outright. Max couldn't hold back the emotions as they came. She was too tired and wrung-out to care if she ugly-cried in front of her friend. Min was always warm to her, respectful; however Max hadn't been aware of this admiration.

"You and I make a great team," she continued. "Each of us props up the other. So Max, when you jump through a ring of exotic metal charged with petawatts of energy, land in an uncertain future where black holes and misogynists and oceans of water are conspiring to kill us? Because you want to save your dog? Bet the farm I'm coming with you."

Days passed. Little changed.

Their bodies continued to heal, and the women answered the cyclical questions from Daft researchers concerning the events that took place in their future. Or their past. It was hard to keep a stable frame of reference.

Min worried that she might lose her mind. She needed to see a normal sky, warm her skin under a healthy, normal sun. Their first weeks home had been nothing except rotating between their suite, Medical, and interviews.

Max wasn't doing much better. Starved for information and bored silly, she got a security detail in their room after disassembling her terminal to bypass the network lockout. At least Neils Bork was here to provide her comfort. At the moment, Min would have paid money for companionship like that.

And Waffel—or Eta, rather—had disappeared. For a couple of days, she was a persistent fixture in their schedule, accompanying them on their round-robin of physical pokes and psychological prods. Then her presence faded. First, she skipped some checkups with Gelding, but gradually her presence faded altogether. The women hadn't seen her in several days.

"Maybe she forgot about us," Max said. "Or nice-girl-Eta was just an act to get us to comply."

Min scooted up on the bed, cramming another pillow behind her aching lower back. "Possible, but I doubt it. She doesn't strike me as that person anymore. I can't say why. I don't have actual evidence, but I get a vibe from her. Like she's worried about us. Not what we could do for her."

"I know what you mean." Max rolled to her side, her hand falling over the edge of the bed, looking for Bork's fur. "The old Dr. Shauna Waffel would have slit our throats if it fit her plans. But Eta, she seems to give a crap about people." Her fingers brushed the soft belly fur over Bork's ribs, prompting the dog to raise his head to lick her arm.

Min agreed in silence.

"Any idea what they're waiting for?" Max asked.

Min's gaze rose from the dog. The engineer frowned with concern. "What do you mean?"

Max gestured at the room. "They can't keep us here forever. We're about to go nuts from boredom and lack of information."

Min smirked, pointing with her chin to the goody box the Daft Institute had provided. "They're trying their best, though, aren't they?" The artifact container had been packed with seven identical sets of clothes for each of them: bleach-white cotton sweatpants, matching tank tops and t-shirts, and what she could only describe as "corporate underwear." The box also contained a few physical books - all fiction, and nothing recent. Min grabbed the copy of Gene Wolfe's *Peace* off her bedside table and held it up. "We have lost years to catch up on, and they give us books we've already read."

The book was a favorite of hers. Each time she read the story, it hit her in a fresh way. But there must be countless new books to consume, and her brain was salivating over the promised flavor of something fresh.

"That's what I mean. They can't shield us from this future forever." Max sat up, her feet dangling over Bork's tush. "Can they?"

Min thought through it again. "I don't see why they would. If anything, they'll share us with the world. The Amelia Earharts of time travel, brought to you by the Daft Institute."

"I'd love it if they realize it soon," Max said. "I need out of this room. Bork needs a real walk."

As if in response, the visitor alert chimed. Min sat up while Max tried to quiet Bork's hackles at the high-pitched noise. "Come in," they sang together.

The magnetic locks on the doors whispered as they retracted, and the door opened. One of their security detail entered the room, then stepped to the side to hold open the door. Eta Waffel followed, carrying two large and steaming tumblers. The odor of toasty roasted coffee arrived in her wake.

"Good morning," Waffel smiled. "Thought you two might enjoy real coffee instead of that fungus water from the cafeteria." She handed them each a mug and pulled creamers and sweeteners out of the pocket of her lab coat and set them on one of the bedside tables.

Min relished the glowing warmth in her hands. Dark and complex scents rose from the liquid. She enjoyed coffee, but it was fresh sensations she craved after so many days of boredom. Max groaned with approval as she loaded up hers with cream and sugar, then took an indulgent swig.

"I know it's been hard, and I apologize for being absent. It was for a good reason. You haven't gone stir crazy?"

"Not yet, but we can see crazy from here," Max joked.

Waffel nodded, lips pressed with regret. "I am sorry. Gathering the folks I need has been more difficult than I expected."

"Any idea when we can get out of here? Start exploring this new future of ours?" Min asked.

Waffel pulled a chair away from the small table in the far corner. She sighed as she sat, the sound of old bones settling. Min saw fresh reminders of their lost time: the extra lines on Waffel's face, the streak of gray waving down the left side of her hair.

"Well, that's why I'm here," she reported. "I've gotten Daft to expand the bounds in which you're allowed to move. You'll still be under constant guard and surveillance. Also, everyone at Daft has explicit orders to not interact with you outside of official interviews. But now you're permitted to go to the cafeteria and the gym whenever you want."

Min's ears perked up. Her antsy body craved a run.

"Can we use the network?" Max asked.

"Soon," Waffel replied. "I want you debriefed before you venture out on your own recognizance. I need to corral three people before we do that. One arrived this morning, the other two should be here later today."

"Who are they?" Min asked.

"Glad you asked," Eta replied. She pulled out a tablet, tapped the interface, and spoke into the screen, "Why don't you come in and introduce yourself."

The door latch clicked, and Min heard it squeak open. Careful, soft steps sounded from the short tile entry, past the bathroom and closet doors.

In her periphery, Min sensed recognition from Max: her eyes widening as she caught the first glimpse of the individual entering their room.

The woman was lanky. As tall as Min at least. Thin but not athletic. The rumpled clothing under her white lab coat was drab and sloppy next to Eta's crisp power outfit. Long hair pulled into a loose bun, with plenty of dangling stragglers that suggested a natural wave. And intelligent eyes set deep over high cheekbones.

Min recognized her from those eyes. The face was older, but the poster in Future-Bruce's workshop had captured her steady and secure gaze perfectly.

"You're Alice Courgette, aren't you?"

40

PATTERN RECOGNITION

The corridors evoked a sense of familiarity and unease. After twelve years, Daft hadn't messed with the building layout or interior design. Every surface remained sterile, clean, and well-maintained; none of it differed from what Min expected. An endless stream of right angles, the starchy pallor broken only by the black placards marking each closed door. The only tangible difference? Every one of them was blacked out. She assumed to hide information from herself and Max.

"So, what is your field of study?" Min asked as they passed another intersection. "What area of physics do you specialize in?"

Alice shook her head, a slight rise coming to the corner of her mouth. "I'm not a physicist. Not really. I have a Psy. D. from the University of Texas, and a Ph. D. in Applied Quantum Neurology from Berkeley."

"Quantum Neurology?" Max echoed.

"Applied Quantum Neurology," she confirmed.

"What is that?" Min asked. "I've never heard of it."

"A young field in the spectrum of the Sciences, but based on some pretty old ideas," Courgette replied. "Most of it concerns quantifying consciousness."

Max and Min walked in ponderous silence; Min glanced at her friend, finding the same stern look of confusion she was experiencing.

"What projects are you working on that are related to our situation?" Min probed.

Alice's smirk widened into a knowing and gentle smile. "I can't tell you about that," she deflected with natural grace. "Not yet. But I promise we'll get there."

"The cafeteria's right up here," Waffel added. "Once we have lunch, the others should be here. Then we'll start your debrief."

Max's calloused fingers weaved into Min's hand, and Min gave her a reassuring squeeze. The engineer had confided her experience in the cafeteria—finding her own murdered corpse. The two women had spent hours talking it through. Max had been desperate to reconcile a timeline where she sees herself dead, then lands in a future where she shouldn't exist. And now, here they were, entering the very space where Future-Max died. Or didn't. Min shunned the temporal dynamics from her mind to ablate the headache they would cause.

Framed in the hallway ahead was a sea of tables and the bobbing currents of people mulling about. Max's palm had grown slick. "It's okay," Min whispered. "You can stay in the room, and I can bring food back."

"I'm okay." Her face twitched, as if the gears churning in Max's mind were pressing against her skin.

"We can leave anytime," Min reminded her. "Just say the word."

Max nodded, and Min led her into the wide space.

The crowd in the expansive area was overwhelming. On a normal day, she might consider it a light flow of folks looking for bites to eat. But, after weeks of solitude, Min now perspired under a glaring spotlight of self-consciousness. Eyes were on them, there was no doubt—the two strangers from Daft's past, walking anachronisms in a future they knew nothing about.

Each woman ordered a familiar dish. Max opted for a bowl of ramen with synthesized protein and plant materials, flavored with luxurious and aromatic green onions that had to be real. Min went for a staple, her I-don't-want-to-think-about-it grilled chicken salad wrap.

The act of making a decision comforted Min, even if it was only a meal. Max's head remained on a pivot trying to watch the entire eatery at once, fearing her future past might find her if she stayed here too long.

Min leaned into her friend and whispered, "Your melon is going to pop off if you keep twisting it around like that."

Max shrugged as she set her bowl on the table in front of her. "I can't help but worry Bruce will jump out from somewhere. And he'll want to murder us."

"It's a reasonable expectation after what we've been through," Min comforted as she took in the room. There were a few dozen folks, all in standard Daft lab coats, scattered throughout the space in twos and threes. It seemed a natural scene for the cafeteria, even familiar; yet as she scoured the people, looking for anyone she recognized, a pattern stuck out to her. Or, rather, a lack of a pattern.

Min turned to her friend, leaned in close, and whispered in her ear as if sharing a secret. "Have we seen *any* men since we arrived here?"

Max stopped sucking up noodles and gave the room another glance as she considered the question.

Before Max answered, fingers gripped Min's shoulder. Her gaze darted up as adrenaline warmed her chest. It was Eta, but that did nothing to calm her frayed nerves.

"The others are here," Eta said with an eager grin. "As soon as you're done eating, let's head up to my office."

41

THE BIG GUNS

The four women sat at a wide conference table in Waffel's executive office, with Min and Max facing the other two. Behind Waffel and Courgette was a wall of darkened windows.

"We'll depolarize the windows after the debriefing, I promise."

Min hadn't asked; Alice must have picked up on her shifting gaze. She liked Courgette. The woman was curious, but fed that curiosity in a sensitive manner, her surgical ability to observe detail tempered by empathy and understanding.

"Thank you," Min replied. "Can we begin? We're both eager to learn what's happened while we were gone."

Alice and Eta offered calm smiles and exchanged a brief glance. Their formal posture and relaxed countenance showed they were ready to spill whatever beans they were holding.

Eta began, "Very well. Let's start with the date. Today is Tuesday, September 23rd. The year is 2036. A smidge over twelve years since you two crossed your Foresight aperture."

Min processed the information in silence. They knew a rough time frame; learning specifics was at once calming and alarming.

"Except…" Waffel's lips tightened as her hands wrung together. "As far as we're concerned, that never happened."

Min didn't understand. Max beat her to the question, blurting out, "What does that mean? That you kept it a secret? Is anyone even aware we've been missing?" A sense of betrayal shaded her voice.

"No, not like that," Waffel explained. "I mean, no one at Daft has knowledge of the Foresight project. We have no record of that quantum optics research here."

"Impossible!" Min crossed her arms. "The Foresight telescope is your design! What the hell is going on here?"

Alice leaned forward, her smile placative. "The thing you need to understand is that these apertures don't operate the way you think."

"Well, that's obvious," Max said, her words dripping with cynicism.

Courgette raised a finger, asking for patience from the women. "I misspoke. What I mean to say is that your understanding of what they do is incorrect. The apertures—they don't just imprint quantum properties. They're not limited to manipulating photons."

"We've realized that," Min prodded.

"Right," Alice continued. "You've experienced first-hand that they can imprint matter. Such as your bodies."

"Again, confirmed." A biting tone clipped Max's words. The engineer was losing her patience.

"The piece you don't comprehend is where the data for the imprint is originating. What do you know about these apertures? The material from which they are made?"

"Exotic metal," Min shrugged.

"We call it Asmodium," Waffel said.

"Asmodium?" Min repeated. "I've never encountered that name." Discomfort seethed in her as she held Waffel's steady gaze. Why had she never questioned what constituted the exotic metal? And why had her advisor never explained this to her before?

"It's an artificial crystalline metal. Assembled from base atoms into a specific structure," Eta added.

"But if Foresight never happened, how do you know what the apertures can do?" Min asked.

Alice spoke up again. "From my research. You asked about my area of study earlier? I aim to understand the quantum nature of thought. The relationship between human consciousness and reality."

Min and Max sat silent, processing the unexpected tangent.

"Asmodium carries a unique property. You appreciate how passing light through charged quartz crystals can produce entangled photons? It sounds like that was part of the Foresight project?"

"It is," Min confirmed. "Or... was."

"Right. Asmodium does something similar. If the crystal arrangement is pristine, and you run enough power through it, the metal imprints the matter and energy passing through it. It *changes* reality."

"Changes reality?" Max scoffed. "Changes it... to what?"

Alice offered a wry smile. "Remember what I said before? That the aperture doesn't work as you think?"

The women nodded, their curiosity radiating like heat.

"At the risk of sounding clever: the apertures work exactly how you *think*. The consciousness in closest proximity becomes the source of the quantum imprinting."

Min pressed into her chair. "You mean, our thoughts..."

"Are turned into reality," Courgette finished Min's reasoning.

A stunned calm came over the women. Min scoured her memories, replayed the incidents of their misadventure.

"I... I screamed at Bruce that I hope he drowned," Min said. "And then he opened a portal that sucked in an ocean."

Alice's eyebrows piqued. "We call that *priming*. Once someone mentions a pink gorilla, you can't stop your mind from processing the pink gorilla. Our consciousness is unable to avoid the concept once it's in there. You've experienced how dangerous priming can be around an aperture. You put the notion in that man's brain—the idea of drowning—and the ring cemented on it. Created reality around it."

"My dog!" Max sat up, palms hitting the table. "I kept daydreaming about Neils Bork, how much I missed him and wanted him back!"

"And the aperture in your lab took you to right to him," Alice said. Silence pressed into the conference room as her gentle gaze shifted from Max to Min and back. "I'm guessing you were also nervous about using a singularity for power, given the reality you experienced?"

Min sighed. "That was Bruce. He kept mansplaining how we could destroy the solar system."

"Priming," Alice repeated. "The human mind is quite susceptible to it. The Asmodium is only an impartial transducer for the Universe's least governable data source."

"Wait," Max countered, "so we didn't travel through time?"

"Not intentionally," Waffel replied. "Our working theory is that the physics of being in the black hole's extreme gravity account for that."

"And so this," Min gestured at everything around them, "this isn't our future? It's just something we conjured up while the building was crashing on top of us?"

Eta and Alice shared another knowing look. Alice's eyes widened, and Waffel nodded as if giving her permission to continue.

"That's where our theories turn bare," Courgette said. "We've always assumed these imprinted realities were artificial, temporary constructs. Created by the Asmodium rings in response to energy and consciousness. Except-"

"Except we came *here*," Min interrupted. "And you're no figment of our imagination. Not an ephemeral creation, are you?"

Alice smiled with warmth and humor, placing a hand on her chest as if clutching pearls. "I don't feel temporary, no. I've existed my whole life."

"But, so have we," Min mumbled. The first pangs of a tension headache reached up from her neck.

"And we saw your photo in that hellacious shithole," Max added. "We were unaware of you before that. There's no way we summoned you up from nothing, twice."

Another nod from Alice. "Indeed. My current thinking is that the Asmodium isn't *creating* reality through quantum imprinting. Instead, it's transferring matter and energy *between* existing universes."

"How in the hell-"

"It's not even a hypothesis yet," Alice interrupted, raising a hand to quiet the women. "And besides, we're already beyond the limits of my expertise."

Waffel continued the thread. "We need help to figure this out. That much is obvious. Thankfully, we have experts on which to call. Former students of ours who've applied this technology to achieve amazing breakthroughs."

"The 'big guns' you keep mentioning?" Min asked.

Eta nodded. "They're the authorities here, pioneers in Asmodium applications. I'm confident they will help us piece this all together. Figure out what we can and should do to help you." She reached a hand across the table. Not an offer of support, but a gathering of the women's attention. "I'm going to invite them in now. You two need to steel yourselves."

Min's eyes locked on to Max, whose gaping stare conveyed the same question itching Min's mind: *steel ourselves for what?*

Alice lifted a small tablet from the conference table; her bony fin-gertip bounced once on the interface. "Enter now, please," she called into the tablet's dark glass.

The latch on the conference room door clicked. Min spun her chair to face the sound. Max's fingers interlocked with hers again in a wad of clammy nerves.

The door eased into the room, and two familiar people entered. Max gasped. Her fingers crushed Min's knuckles, yet the shock at the visage in the doorway washed away the discomfort of Max's death grip.

"Min, Max," Waffel said, "allow me to introduce Chief Scientist Minerva Draper, and Distinguished Engineer Maxine Cantros."

ΛUTHOR'S ΝOTℓ

If you enjoyed this book, you're going to love the next installment of the story! Don't miss out—join my newsletter to receive updates as Gradient Descent: Theory of Anything approaches publication!

• • • ● • ● • ● • •

Please review *Gradient Descent: Schrödinger's Dog*. Leaving a review helps make this book more discoverable by the right readers. The ones like you, with the big brains, a well-developed sense of humor, and fantastic taste in reading material. Having more of those readers motivates and promotes my writing career.

Thank you for reading this story. I hope it was a page-turner that left you thinking and laughing. If you'd like to know when my next book will be available, please visit my author website: https://www.jim-christopher.com. There, you can subscribe to my mailing list. In exchange, you'll get access to free stories and resources available nowhere else—such as discussion guides for book clubs and chapters that never made it into the final draft.

Interested in bringing this story into your book club? I have a discussion guide available. I am also happy to chat about the book with your group; simply reach out using the contact form on my website.

• • • ● ● • ● ● • • •

After working for decades in technology, I've witnessed all of the blatant and institutional misogyny represented in this book (except the ones that involve fictional weapons from the future). In fact, the core idea for Gradient Descent congealed while listening to my wife talk through the non-work struggles of her work day. In our technology careers, she and I have the same problems to solve, but her obstacles far outnumber mine, and they're pointless and juvenile.

So, I thought: *What if we take that kind of behavior to an extreme? What if the last men and women on Earth are co-workers? Would they work together to survive? Would misogyny outlive an apocalypse?*

Seven months later, you're holding this book.

It took me years to learn that not acknowledging this behavior when it happens makes me a quiet part of the problem. That not speaking up in the moment is a privilege. I figured out pretty quickly that my wit is a powerful resource for those who need it. I don't mean that I am unkind to those acting out of bounds—at least not always. Instead, my sense of humor and observation skills can create safe opportunities for women to be themselves and, if they choose, to clap-back.

One story in particular I wanted to include in the book so, so badly. It didn't fit, though. It would have required a significant shift in environment and characters, and I decided it was too unwieldy for Gradient Descent's tight marriage of plot and setting. That said, as the author of the book, I have the privilege of writing this backmatter. So, here's that story I wanted to fold in, but couldn't...

My first "real" job was pretty amazing. I worked with a bunch of smart people doing smart things. Space things. And optics, kind of like Min and Max in the book you're reading now. Of course, my role on this team was meager, if necessary—I helped the documentation team capture the smart things that other people were doing—but it was still exhilarating to be around that stuff. Space telescopes, satellites, cell phones, automotive components—this team helped design countless useful, world-changing, and mind-blowing pieces of technology.

One evening, we are out celebrating something—a release, perhaps? Maybe a project wrap-up? There's definitely drinking and no-goodnicking, which helps explain my inability to recall the context. A woman on the engineering team—we shall call her "Mary" although that's not her name—had a very sharp sense of humor and keen hearing, both of which come into play in this tale.

An outside-of-work friend happens into the same hotel bar where my inside-of-work friends are imbibing. Let's call this friend "Joe," which is not his real name, either. Over the course of an hour, Joe hits on Mary so hard I wonder if she owes him money. I watch from a bar stool several meters away while he verbally peacocks around her, trying to gain attention and favor with inflated stories of his mundane graduate school work.

Mary is unimpressed, and Joe takes the hint.

He rejoins me at the bar. I ask, "So, what do you think of Mary? She's awesome, right?" Because Mary *is* awesome. Intelligent and creative as they come, brilliant engineer, and funny as hell. She runs marathons. Climbs cliffs. Spends her weekends saving beached whales (at least she would, I think; there are not a lot of beached whales in the desert of Arizona).

Joe sighs and says (his voice loud enough that Mary could hear three seats away), "I mean, she's cute. But she's no rocket scientist."

I laugh that obnoxious laugh you may have heard if you know me personally. Joe wants to know why. So I spin on my stool and shout, "Hey Mary, remind us. What is it you do for a living?"

She downs the remnants of her beer, slams the stein on the bar, and stands to meet Joe square in the eye. As she hoists on her leather jacket, snapping the collar for effect, she says:

"I'm a fucking rocket scientist."

And the best part? It's true. 100% honest. She does rockets for a living. A literal rocket scientist that designs safe ways to send the things we build into space.

Ego Joe hadn't asked. Never bothered himself with the details of her person. Absorbed with getting in her pants, which—I'm sorry Joe—were way too grown-up for you to be playing with.

This occurred in the late 1990s. The first time I penned this observed event was in a blog post celebrating Ada Lovelace Day on October 13, in the heyday of my technology career, say, around 2013. My daughters were young, and I dedicated time to teach them how women like Ada have had a profound impact on society. Having that history is vital for them, I think—in particular, understanding how the technical contributions from women are under-celebrated and often downplayed. So I want them to know about Ada and Marie and Lise and Jane and Rosalind and as many others as I can find. To understand their contributions. To acknowledge that we owe them for my career and our family's well-being. To give my kids high expectations of themselves.

But I know it's a longshot that history lessons will have a tangible effect. I mean, why should I expect stories of Ada to have a significant impact on my girls, when similar stories about C.S. Babbage had milquetoast effects on me when I was their age? Interesting, necessary, but not enough to light their fuse.

This is why I hold a constant torch to find Marys. Living people for my daughters to witness striving towards real and amazing accomplishments every day. Folks that can converse about their wonders and interests. People my daughters can see themselves becoming.

Sure, I want them to know that "once upon a time there was Ada, and she set the stage to bring computer programming into creation."

But bearing witness to Mary? Right here, right now, kicking science's ass? That has a profound impact on their mindset. Because believing you can accomplish a thing is a prerequisite to achieving the thing. And as the saying goes, seeing is believing.

All of which is my long-winded way of reiterating the adage: *representation matters.* In art. In science. In education. In occupation, governance, politics, and community. In life.

· • • ● • ● • • ·

If you'd like to learn more about becoming an effective ally for women and other under-represented groups in the workplace, I invite you to explore the following resources:

- HeForShe: https://www.heforshe.org/en

- LeanIn: https://leanin.org/tips/workplace-ally#

- This HBR article: https://hbr.org/2018/10/how-men-can
  -become-better-allies-to-women

ACKNOWLEDGMENTS

It would be wrong to start this barrage of gratitude anywhere other than Julie Smith. Working in tech is hard enough. Shifting priorities, businesses that act like psychopaths, and an amoebic technological landscape that requires constant learning. Watching her deal with all of that, plus the senseless bullshit that comes with being a woman in the field, has been a significant part of my drive to write this book. My appreciation of her talent, patience, and grace grows every single day. I love you; I like you; and I think you're pretty great. We should move in together and get serious about our relationship.

Special thanks to Rie Merrit, on several fronts. For bringing data to the conversation. For tirelessly prioritizing WIT in the community. And for contributing to the curated list of allyship resources included in the backmatter of this book. As your official mansplainer-of-record, I am at your disposal.

My deepest gratitude to Liz Dunbar for the constant enthusiasm and impromptu line edit. And of course for the life-long friendship that I don't deserve.

Admiration to Bree Smith, who did the thing even though it was scary and contained misteaks. I am proud of you.

Love to my beta and ARC readers: Audrey, Liz, Ann, Pamela Anne, Kristen, Alan, Bernice, John, Joyce, Beverly, Nicole, and Juanita. The feedback may have been intense, scary to offer, but y'all made everything in the book better. Thank you for your support, indulgence, and honesty.

And thanks to the Jiminions who read and respond to my monthly newsletter. You provide that connection to my readers that makes this dream feel like real life.

And, it would be wrong to end my gratitude anywhere other than my daughters. Kids[0] and kids[1], you are the human burritos over-stuffed with my ambitions and fears. You kindle hope that the reign of old straight white men is ending. That their flaccid obsessions will turn obsolete in a world filled with the likes of you and your generation. I really hope I'm like you when I grow up.

About the Author

Jim Christopher lives in Decatur, Georgia. His career has been a crooked path, meandering through stagehand, audio engineer, carpenter, cognitive psychologist, behavioral researcher, musician, software developer, learning sciences advisor, to whatever he might be doing today.

He writes speculative fiction, suspense, thrillers, science fiction, and horror. His debut novel *Season of Waiting* was named a finalist in the American Fiction Awards, and the follow-up *Sick as our Secrets* won First Place in the BookFest Awards for Supernatural Thrillers.

To relax, Jim crochets, builds tiny houses, walks his dog, reads, and tries to stay active. His guilty pleasures include laughing, petit fours, end-of-the-world movies, and escape rooms.

More from Jim Christopher

The Utopian Testament

Season of Waiting

Killdeer

Sick as our Secrets

This is Goodbye for Now

Cult of Possibility

Gradient Descent

Gradient Descent: Schrödinger's Dog

Gradient Descent: Theory of Anything

Standalone Novels

See Red

Visit https://www.jim-christopher.com for the latest news!